I0653755

Protecting what's Mine

A MAPLE SMALL TOWN ROMANCE
BOOK 3

Jessica Whaley

Protecting what's Mine

Copyright © 2025 Jessica Whaley
All Rights Reserved.

Cover Art: Jessica Whaley
Editor: Pat Norton

Publisher:
Jessica Whaley
P.O. Box 785
Leesburg, Al. 35983

ISBN (Paperback): 979-8-9906151-9-9
ISBN (Ebook): 979-8-9906151-8-2

Dedication:

For the ones who want a love that will meet you in your darkest place and lead you towards the light.

Protecting what's Mine

Protecting what's Mine

Author's Note:

While this is not the end of the Maple Series, this is the end for The Mapleson kiddos. I saved Collin's book for last because he seemed to be everyone's favorite.

This book does not contain a third act breakup, but it does hit on darker elements.

This series is what started it all for me. I remember sitting at my kitchen bar, writing Letters to Magnolia – before I knew it was going to be The Maple Series.

Contrary to popular belief, when I was writing the first book, the other two were not on my radar. I had never written a book before and was not sure I would even get it done.

Even if I did, I thought LTM was going to be the only one and I would go onto another standalone.

Then I got feedback from beta and ARC readers and quickly realized I had not only built a memorable MFC and MMC, but I also had side characters who everyone fell in love with too.

I look back on that first book and think, *Dang, there is so much I wished I had done differently.* But then I look back at the growth within my writing and it makes me thankful for that starting point.

Thank you for loving these characters as much as I have loved writing them.

Protecting what's Mine

Each one has their own spin of me in them – or aspects of my childhood (although there were changes and rearrangements for fictional purposes).

You cannot go into this story blind. The first two books must be read first to understand the timeline, characters, and town.
The timeline of this book relates to Book 2, The Light in his Darkness.

I started this book the way I did for a couple reasons: You already know about Alyssa and Collin in The Light in his Darkness and I wanted to see what it would be like to write a book within the same timeline as the other one. If you don't like it, don't tell me. ;)

As you know Collin is the goofball of the kids, but you may not have seen before now, he is also all man. Who leads with confidence to protect what is his.

Alyssa – her past is what nightmares are made of. I won't sugarcoat it; she has been through so much grief and heartache that it's enough to make anyone question their life.
But the once weak and terrified girl turns in a powerful woman who decides she is tired of being the victim to her circumstances.

I will say it again; **DO NOT GO INTO THIS BOOK BLIND. Please read the prior two before proceeding.**

Protecting what's Mine

Now, enjoy the sexy and greedy Collin Jeffrey Mapleson.

Protecting what's Mine

This book contains trigger warnings.
I trust that you know your triggers before starting this
book.

This book contains the following triggers:
Graphic sexual content and adult language.
A narcissist ex, abusive past (for fmc) such as sexual abusive and losing twin
sister.
Murder (self-defense)

Protecting what's Mine

Protecting what's Mine

Prologue
Collin

The sun is setting behind the fall mountains here in Maple, Georgia. A light breeze is felt signaling Winter won't be long.

Megan and Grandmother are in the house cooking supper while Grandfather and I decided to ride the pasture lines this evening to check fences.

I sit on the back of one of our mares while Grandfather sits in his saddle beside me on one of his favorite geldings.

His smile is as wide as the Grand Canyon as he looks over the land before us.

I cannot imagine how much pride he feels looking over a piece of property he worked so hard for.

Our pastures are full of horses, cattle, and other smaller livestock. The creeks and ponds are flowing rapidly from the storms we had a few days ago and off in the distance, the birds are heard chirping their last songs before Winter arrives.

Slowly, things will be changing, as the seasons transition. We see it every year; the trees and flowers go dormant, the animals put on heavy winter coats, the grass turns to mud.

It is a time where we also slow down and still ourselves for the upcoming Spring and Summer.

But the hardest change I have seen lately is that of the mind of the man who raised me.

He is one of the strongest men I know and one that I respect more than anyone else.

I don't know how much longer we will have him here with us. He has become a lot for my grandmother to take care of.

Megan and I try to help as much as we can, but the farm is a lot of work within itself, too.

It's odd though; he is more like himself in the saddle than anywhere else. Our rides along these hills I will cherish for years to come.

"I am proud of you, son," he tells me, catching me off guard.

I look at him, fighting back tears. It seems they only come when he says things like this.

"You are becoming a man, and I am not stupid Collin, I know I am not the man I used to be. Things are changing with me."

"I don't think any different of you, Grandfather," I assure him.

He smirks, "Good because I could still kick your ass."

And that he could.

"There are some things I need to tell you before I slip into my other mind again."

I sit up straighter, not sure I want to hear what he has to say.

"One day, you are going to find a woman that you want to share this life with. You will cherish the ground she walks on, and you will be willing to put your own life on the line when it comes to her."

He never looks at me, but his voice is hoarse. "I found that in your grandmother. We came from two different lives and at one time, your great granddaddy did not want her dating me."

I perk up; *I had no idea.*

"It's a long story son, and honestly one I don't care to relive. But I never gave up on her. On us."

I smile. My grandparents are the reason I believe in true love. I only hope I find that someday.

"You might turn your nose up at it now, but one day when you hear your child's heartbeat for the first time," he pauses and turns to me, "That is the day you truly become

14

a man. Please don't ever let the family you come from destroy the family you make. The day you find someone you want to make a home with, they become your priority. Not your grandmother and me, and not your sister. You and the one you pick for forever is your number one besides your children."

I'm shocked at his words. "But you always said family is the most important thing."

He nods. "I have and it is. You help your sister when she needs you. But never take away from you and your home to do so." He looks back across the land. "So many kids now days are quick to listen to those opinions who don't walk in their shoes. Divorces are easy, son. Leaving when it gets hard is not the right move. Staying, that is the right thing to do. Working together through the good, bad, and downright ugly."

"How did you and grandma get through the things you did?" I ask.

He chuckles. "I learned to shut up and listen."

I smirk. "And everything worked out for the best."

His smile turns serious. "That woman had every reason to leave me. And I even told her once she should have. Our parents didn't make it easy. The war didn't either. Life was hard during our time. But I learned in the process that she was the one who mattered, no one else. So, I shut up and listened to her. She is a smart woman. Most of them are. If men would stop being so prideful, maybe more marriages would last."

His hand goes to my shoulder, and he squeezes it. "I may not be here to see you become the man for your own home someday. But remember, you are the protector. You are the one at the frontlines. And you protect everything that is yours with your whole being."

I nod at him, tears glistening in my eyes.

"Yes sir."

"Good." He smirks. "And for what it's worth, your parents would be so proud of you and your sister. You two have been through more than most adults in their entire life; yet here you are pushing on with laughter and strength. That's because you are a Mapleson. We dodge those curveballs."

My grandmother's favorite saying warms my heart; because it's true, life's worth dodging curve balls for.

"Another thing," he starts. "Don't be sad when I am gone. Live your life, Collin. You will always have this farm. But don't forget to go out and live, too."

"This farm is my home," I tell him, and he chuckles.

"This will always be your home. My dream was always to have a place where my children and grandchildren could be safe and loved."

His face turns serious. "But you are only young once, Collin. Live it. When you get to be an old man like me, you realize quickly how much time you waste worrying about things that don't matter. Life is so beautiful and it's all at your fingertips."

I smile. "There's nowhere else I rather be than here."

He nods. "I hope you and your sister continue to love it and raise your own families on it. I will be watching from the best seat up above, smiling down."

Chapter One
Collin

"Come for me like a good girl."

She moans into my shoulder while I have her back pressed against the shower wall and my dick inside her. From the first moment I laid eyes on her, she captivated me. But something else entirely took over me, too; she seemed like a lost duckling, and I wanted nothing more than to scoop her up and make her feel at home in my arms.

"Collin I-I'm going to . . ."

And she does, all over my cock, milking me into my sweet release. I hold us steady with my hands on the wall of the shower beside her head as she goes limp in my arms. Our breathing is labored, coming down from the high we were just on.

She has been timid lately when it comes to sex, and I am not sure why. If she does not initiate it, then it does not happen. I want to know what is going on in that pretty head of hers, but I don't push. When she is ready, she will tell me.

"You are going to make me late for work."

I smirk, "You could have said no."

Her legs unwrap from my torso, and she finds her footing again, grabbing her washcloth to wash her body before leaving. "Collin Mapleson, who would say no to you?"

I bend down near her neck, raking my teeth over her ear and whisper, "You, my love. You could get me to do whatever you want."

Turning to face me she smiles innocently. "And don't you forget it."

Stepping out of the shower, I leave her to get ready for the day. I have things to do myself. My sister is coming home from her rodeo tour and our cousin and best friend have just had their baby.

An uneasiness hits me, I sure hope Megan is in a good mood. I have not told her about my relationship with Alyssa and if anyone is going to have anything to say about it, it will be her.

I love my sister; she basically raised me, but letting go is not her strong suit.

Years ago, when I was just a little boy, our parents died in a horrible car crash with our uncle, killing them all upon impact. Since then, Megan has taken it upon herself to be my parent. Although we did live with our wonderful grandparents, Megan still thought she was in control of me.

Unfortunately, even being twenty-five now, my wings are still clipped.

"Collin?"

"Yeah, babe?"

"Should I expect to see you tonight?"

I take a deep breath; the two most important women in my life must meet eventually, I am just not sure when the best time will be.

"Yeah. Just let me spend some time with Megan. I got some stuff to do at the ranch, too. I will be back over later tonight."

"Guess I have to get use to sharing you now." She winks at me. "I hope she likes me."

Walking into the bathroom, I wrap my arms around her waist, pulling her into me, resting my head on her shoulder.

"She does not have a choice. You are mine."

***

The view of **Magnolia Farm** stirs a sense of home in my chest when I turn down the driveway. Pastures full of horses and cattle on both sides of the road as my tires raise dust behind me.

This place is every bit of what made me the man I am today, and I hope to show my girl around here someday soon.

Pulling my truck up to the white farmhouse that my grandparents raised us in, Reba, Izzy, and George all run off the porch to meet me.

"Hey pups." I give them all their own scratches before heading down to the barn for morning chores.

Opening the large rolling door of the barn, the sunlight fades inside, showing me faces waiting on their morning breakfast.

"Molly and Tiny, how is it that you always know when breakfast time is? There are no clocks in this barn." I laugh and take the time to give them both scratches.

Flipping the switch on in the tack room where we keep our feed, I grab feed buckets and start scooping feed into each one.

The neighs in the hallway start to get louder as our four-legged children start to get impatient; I swear they are equivalent to toddlers.

"Here you go, heathens," I huff, pouring feed into Tiny's bucket and make my way over to Molly.

The rest of my time is spent filling up water and feed for the other horses and cattle.

Looking at my watch, I let out a big breath. Megan had texted me last night that she would be here by now. It's well past six o'clock.

Pulling out my phone, I type in her number and hold the phone to my ear with my shoulder while I finish watering everyone.

"Hello?" Her voice rings through.

"Where the hell are you?"

I can practically see her rolling her eyes just from my tone. Getting her feathers ruffled is one of my favorite pastimes.

"I just entered Maple."

I am about to say something about how she is never on time, but a loud bang takes over my thoughts.

"Megan what was . . ."

"Collin, I got to go! I just got hit in the side of the horse trailer!"

And she hangs up. My heart goes to my feet; *our parents died from a car crash.*

Rushing to finish filling up everyone's water, I drop the water hose and run to the faucet to turn it off.

I redial her number multiple times, trying my best not to panic, but every time it goes to voicemail.

Do not panic. She is fine. She is fine. She is fine.

But calming down is not an option when you lost your parents to a car crash. It reminds you things can change in a split second.

Grabbing my keys, I run to my truck.

Right before I put it in reverse to go find her, my phone rings, "You cannot tell me you have been in a wreck and then hang up!" I yell not giving her a chance to speak, and once I release a big breath that I had no idea I was even holding. "I was about to come look for you!"

"I am okay. CJ is okay. We are about to turn on the driveway now."

"I will meet you in the barn and help you unload, and then we can head to the hospital."

We end our call, and I place my phone back in my pocket when I jump out of my truck, making my way back to the barn.

I swear, some days I want to strangle her, but she is one of my best friends and I don't know what I would ever do without her.

I am back inside the barn when I hear her truck and trailer pull in. The dogs all go running to meet her and Molly's ears perk up. Everyone else is chopped liver when Megan is around.

"Yeah, yeah, we are all happy she is home." I tell all the animals making my way to the back of the trailer to get Crackerjack, the horse Megan rodeos on, out of the trailer.

Stepping into the back of trailer, I grab his halter and guide him backward onto the fresh lawn. "Come on big guy. I got water and feed in your stall ready for you."

CJ knows exactly where his stall is, and he seems happy to be home and back with his buddies.

Tiny's ears lift when he sees him, and they both talk to each other for a few minutes.

I can only imagine they are discussing their last few weeks and filling the other one in on what they missed.

After sliding his halter off his head, I walk out, leaving CJ to eat his breakfast, shutting the stall door behind me making sure it latches.

"You ready?" I ask Meg walking out of the barn. "They are waiting on us."

"Do you know the gender yet?" She grins at me anxiously. We are both excited for our new baby cousin.

"They wanted to tell us together." I shrug as we both walk to my truck and jump inside.

Chapter Two
Alyssa

"Table nine just got seated. Will you take his order for me, Alyssa? I have my hands full at the bar."

I nod at Lexie, who is the best coworker I could ever ask for—she is also becoming a good friend of mine—and grab my pen and note pad out of my waitress apron.

The breakfast rush this morning has left us all worn out and thankfully we are starting to transition to the lunch menu.

Striding up to the table where a guy sits alone, his back to me, I put on my best waitress smile. "Good morning, welcome to Patsy's, what can I get you to drink?"

The brim of his baseball cap hides his face until he looks up, and my knees almost give out from under me.

"Hey, Sugar." His deep tone makes me want to flee.

How did he find me?

"What's wrong, sweetheart? Cat got your tongue?"

I hope he cannot tell my whole body is vibrating with adrenaline right now.

"Kyle. What are you doing here?"

He chuckles, more of an evil laugh if you ask me. I know that tone, he's getting angry. And his anger is the whole reason my body is in the state of wanting to flee at the moment.

"I have been looking for you, of course. Baby, I want you to come home. This place is not you."

This man is psychotic; he is not my fiancé anymore.

The once nice man I thought I fell in love with turned into a sadistic son of a bitch who almost made me end it all.

"Kyle, how did you find me?"

He pounds his fist on the table, making me jump. "Damn it, Alyssa. Stop playing this stupid game and let's go home."

Home? His home hasn't been my home in nearly six months.

A tear slips out of my eye and falls down my cheek; I haven't told Collin about him yet.

His eyes go to my shaky hand that holds my pen but when they soar back into mine, they are black.

Shit. He saw my tattoo.

"What do the letters CM mean?"

Stepping back, I shake my head, "Please leave, Kyle."

"Everything alright, miss?" An older gentleman, wearing a cowboy hat, cowboy boots, and wrangler jeans, in a dark grey button-up walks over to me. His eyes roam from Kyle to myself.

"Why don't you mind your business, old fucker." Kyle's tone is clipped and stern.

That's when the man turns to the side, his hand on a pistol strapped to his hip. "Young man, what you need to do is leave this young woman alone. Or I can promise you, it will not be a good day for you."

Kyle stands abruptly and the force of it nearly makes me fall onto the table I did not even realize I was leaning against.

"I will be in touch." He snarls at me and storms out of the building.

The old man turns to me and grabs my shoulder, "Miss, are you okay? Would you like me to call the cops?"

"N-No," I stutter, "I am fine. He is just an old friend that cannot take a hint."

The man smiles at me, "Get you one of these." He pats the gun that's on his hip. "Men like him fear them. All you have to do is show it and they run off with their tail between their legs."

I grin, thankful for his help.

What I don't tell him, or anyone else, is I do have one at home, loaded and ready for the fear of him finding me and doing something worse than he did before.

"Here." The older gentleman takes out his wallet and hands me a one-hundred-dollar bill, "Put it toward something that will make you smile. Have a good day, miss." And he walks away from me, raising his hat to those he tells bye, and once out the door, is he gone.

"Alyssa, are you okay?" Lexie runs up to me rubbing my shoulder.

"Yeah," I wipe my eye. "Just some guy who got too big for his britches."

She smiles, "Why don't you go ahead and take your break. I will cover the floor."

I grin, appreciating the gesture and decide to take her up on her offer.

Hitting the breakroom door as quickly as I can and locking it; I find the nearest chair and pull my knees up to my chest.

This cannot be happening; how did he find me?

I was smart. I did not leave a trail.

He should not have been able to find me.

I rock in my seat – *I just want him gone.*

Ring Ring.

My phone in my apron starts vibrating, startling me.

Collin

My heart rate immediately starts to calm down by his name alone. But I cannot tell him about Kyle, *not yet.*

"Hey" I try my best to sound peppy.

"Hey babe. How is working going? I didn't bother you, did I?"

"Oh, no. I took an early break. How is the newest Mapleson?"

"Going to be hell on wheels, or should I say four legs, once he's hold enough to hang out with his favorite uncle."

I giggle, "You aren't his uncle, Collin. You are his cousin."

"Potato, Tomato. Or whatever that saying is."

I chuckle, leave it to this goofy man to put me in a better mood and not even know it.

"What time can I expect to see you tonight?" I ask. Honestly, I am hoping he gets there before I do. If Kyle knows where I work now, then he most likely already knows where I live.

"I have a few chores to finish up around the farm and then I was going to go over a little early and cook you some supper if that's okay."

My whole body relaxes.

I smile, my thoughtful *gentleman.*

"And once I get you good and fed, I'll feed you something else."

Now I am full-on giggling.

Leave it to Collin Mapleson to take something so sweet and turn it dirty.

"Sounds good. Need me to get anything when I get off?"

"No, pretty girl. Just get home safely and I will see you there."

"Bye, goofball." I tell him before we disconnect.

Chapter Three
Collin

Alyssa's apartment is smelling like a five-star Italian restaurant while I stir the spaghetti sauce and watch the noodles boil.

I ran to the market on my way here and grabbed everything I need to cook. Alyssa's apartment is filled with nothing but sodas, candy, and chips. I seriously worry about what the girl ate before I came along.

It's been a fantastic day spending time with some of my favorite people and meeting my new little cousin. He is the spitting imagine of my two best friends, and I could not be happier for them.

Megan questioned me as I was leaving the farm earlier and I lied, telling her that I was going to stay at some buddy's house tonight.

I know I need to tell her about my and Alyssa's relationship soon but today was going so well; I did not want to ruin it.

My head turns slightly to the door of Alyssa's apartment when I hear the lock turn. My beautiful girl comes walking through. Poor thing looks exhausted after her shift today.

"Hey babe." I turn the stove down and walk over to her, kissing her on the lips lightly.

"Hey. Something smells good." She smiles, turning and locking the door after sitting her bags down.

"Cooking your favorite tonight," I wink.

"So, some de la Collin Mapleson?" she grins, but her eyes tell me something else. She is not all here right now. Her mind is somewhere in left field.

"What is wrong?" I pull her into me, looking into her eyes.

Her eyes widen. "Oh nothing. Just a long shift is all."

"Well, why don't you go get a shower and I will get supper on the table so you can eat."

She nods, "Sounds perfect."

Her footsteps halt halfway down the hall to her bathroom, and she turns around appearing before me, "Are you staying tonight?"

"Would you like me to?" I grin.

She nods, but I don't miss the way her body relaxes when I nod, "Yes pretty girl. I am staying the night. My bag of clothes is in the bedroom."

I don't know if it was the air kicking on or if I heard her take a long exhale once she turned back down the hall.

A few moments later, I hear the shower come on in the bathroom and I sigh, *what I would give right now to run in there and shower with her.*

One of my favorite places to be. Fortunately for her, if I ran in there and forgot the food, we would starve, and I would most likely burn this place down.

Judging by the look of exhaustion on her face, she needs me to focus on having her food done before I think about my own selfish wants.

Grabbing a wine glass from her cabinets, I open a bottle of white wine I grabbed from the market on my way over and pour her a hefty glass.

I almost get the top screwed back on and decide I want a glass, too. So, I grab me one out of the cabinet to fill one up for myself.

"You are just going to have to deal with me, wet hair and all." Her voice comes into the kitchen, and I turn around to see her in a two-piece lounge set that I love so much. It's hot pink and matches her blonde hair and skin so perfectly.

"I love your hair when you let it dry naturally," I admit.

"Is that for me?" she gestures to the wine glass on the counter.

"Yes ma'am. Figured you would want some to go with your supper."

She smiles, taking a sip and then walking up to me, raising up on her tiptoes and planting a soft kiss to my lips. "Thank you," she whispers before walking over to the dining table.

"You just sit down and relax, and I will bring you a plate," I order her.

"Now this, I could get used to," she jokes taking another hefty sip of her drink. "So where does your sister think you are right now?"

I sigh, "A buddy's house."

"Collin," she huffs.

"I know. I know. I need to tell her. And it is nothing toward you at all. I just know how my sister can be, and I do not want her to run you off."

"Collin, I am not mad. I just don't think you need to keep it from her. If she finds out from anyone else or anyone in town, she will be more upset than you ever thought she could be."

I nod, agreeing. "You don't understand though. Megan is . . . territorial."

"It's only because she loves you." She wipes a tear and now I feel bad. "I would give anything to have Haley back. Please never take having her in your life and your relationship with her for granted."

Haley was her older sister who passed away in a tragic house fire a little over a year ago and she talks about her often.

"I know she is my sister, and I do love her, but you come before anyone else, Alyssa. I want this. I want a life with you. That means you become a priority over everyone, and I won't let them come between us," I assure her.

She nods. "And while I do agree, there's a healthy way for all of this to happen and work out. We can be together, and you can still have Megan in your corner. I would love to have a relationship with her one day, too."

"Oh god. I don't know if I could handle both of you teaming up on me."

She giggles and it makes my heart skip a few beats. That sound is my favorite noise on earth.

Grabbing a plate out of the cabinet, one for me and her, I fix our plates full of spaghetti and toast with a side salad and set them down on the table.

I watch her take a few bites and give me a thumbs up. A sense of pride runs through me; I have never wanted to cook for someone else before.

Not until now.

Bang Bang.

"Alyssa! Open up!!" A male's voice is heard at the front door and my girl looks like she has seen a ghost.

"Alyssa, what is wrong." I ask, the banging hits again but this time harder, "Who is that?'

"Collin . . . I need to tell you something."

"Alyssa, I swear to god if you do not open this door, I will bust it down!!"

Now I am pissed. I do not care who this fucker is, he will not be leaving here in anything but a body bag if he doesn't calm down.

I never saw her leave the room but when I look up, I see my girl coming from her bedroom, a 9mm pistol in her hand.

"Collin … you are about to meet my worst nightmare."

Chapter Four
Alyssa

I have never used this gun before. I purchased it after moving away from home when Kyle and I split up.

Something about the threats he made toward me made me want to feel more safe than sorry.

"Who is on the other side of the door?" Collin asks, a little annoyed.

And I cannot say I blame him. This is a part of my life I never wanted him to know about or have to deal with. I wish more than anything I could go back to the day I met the guy on the other side of the door and turn the opposite way.

The day I met him, he put on show—is that not what all narcissists do?

I know that now.

The banging gets louder, and I know for certain he will kick the door down if someone doesn't open it.

But my whole body is shaking with fear, and I cannot feel my legs.

"Is he a threat?" Collin asks coming up to me, grabbing my hand the pistol is in and taking the gun from my hand.

When I nod, he checks the gun over and places it in the waistband of his jeans before he gently grabs my arm, "Babe. I want you to go in the bedroom right now. Lock the door and keep your phone with you."

He kisses my forehead, "It'll be okay. I will handle it."

Pulling a knife from his pocket he hands it to me, "Just in case."

"Collin, please do not let him past the door."

"I won't. Just try to calm down and get in the bedroom."

I nod, taking a deep breath and walking as quickly as I can to my bedroom, shutting and locking the door behind me.

**

Collin

I have some questions for Alyssa later but right now, the guy at the front door seems like a bigger priority.

I have never seen Alyssa so upset and the fact that she had a gun makes me question how bad this guy can get.

"Alyssa, I know you are home. I followed you here!" the voice says and that lights a fire in my ass.

Grabbing the door and swinging it open, I eye the person on the other side.

He looks about my age, maybe a little older. And without knowing anything about him I can tell he is from the city in his fancy shirt and jeans, clean cut beard and dark short kept hair that is hidden by a baseball cap, with a watch on his wrist that most likely cost more than my truck.

"May I help you?" I ask him calmly.

"Who the fuck are you?" he sneers.

"The better question is who the hell are you and what are you doing banging on a woman's door this late in the evening and threatening her if she doesn't open it?"

His eyes narrow in at me, "It's none of your business."

"It's every bit of my business and apparently you are not welcome here or you would have a key."

"I need to speak to Alyssa. I know she is here," he tells me.

"And that does not mean you get to speak with her if she doesn't want to speak with you." I assure him, my gaze never leaving his.

"Is she fucking you or something?" His tone is more clipped this time which makes me smirk.

"You have a hard time respecting a woman and her boundaries, don't you?" I lean up against the door frame.

He steps toward me. "Don't you dare patronize me."

I lean off the door frame and step toward him this time, my nose almost touching his and when my eyes don't blink, he eventually gives in and backs down.

"I would advise you to get the hell off this property right now before I call the police. And if I were you, I would heed my warning." I take another step toward him. "You don't look like the kind who is from here, but we all take care of each other around these mountains. We don't take too kindly for women to get mistreated either."

He backs off from the door and puts his hands up, "Look man I just needed to talk to her. I'll come back later."

It only takes me two steps to reach him again before I grab the gun out of my back and wave it at him, "If you know what is good for you. You will stay the fuck away from her."

He gulps and walks backwards down the path to his car, jumping inside, and squealing tires as he drove off in a hurry.

Hmm, not sure what got into him. Shame he had to leave in a hurry, I just made supper.

My smirk never leaves my face walking back inside and locking the door behind me.

"Is he gone?" Alyssa enters the living room from the hallway.

"He is." I nod, handing her pistol to her. "Go put it up and come back in here so we can talk."

Her tear-filled eyes hold mine for a moment before nodding and walking back into her bedroom.

While she is gone, I pull out my phone and shoot a text to my buddy, Cade, who is a deputy for the town's sheriff department.

Protecting what's Mine

Hey buddy, are you on shift tonight?

Cade: Yes sir. What's up?

Just curious. There was a guy showed up tonight at Alyssa's apartment. Up to no good. Do you mind having the guys keep an eye on her place for the time being. I am about to get more information from her. He seemed to know her and would not take no for an answer until I showed him I was armed.

Cade: You got it brother. I am on patrol tonight; I will swing by a few times when I am not busy. What does he drive?

Could not really tell in the dark but looked like a black or dark color sedan.

Cade: That really narrows it down. Let me know what you find out from her. Stay safe man.

I will. Thanks, brother. You, too.

I lay my phone on the table in front of the couch and look up to see Alyssa's worried eyes staring into mine, holding a blanket around her shoulders.

"Come here." I pat the cushion beside me on the couch.

She slowly makes her way to me, sitting down, and pulling her feet under her.

My girl is normally so outgoing, energetic, and happy. It hurts my heart seeing her like this.

"He was not supposed to find me," she whispers.

For a moment I almost say what comes to mind, but I decide to sit in silence and let her get her emotions out. Her body shakes beside me and from her sniffles, I know she is crying.

"I am so sorry, Collin. I should have told you about all of this before now. I was just scared."

My arm snakes around her backside and I pull her into my lap, holding her close and kissing the side of her head. I don't care that she kept something from me; all I care about is her feeling safe and for some reason this fucker makes her afraid.

"I can't fix it unless you tell me what I need to know," I tell her calmly.

She sighs. "If I tell you this, promise me you won't kill him yourself."

And by that statement alone, I already know I am not going to like what I hear.

"Collin, please promise me," she says again after I stay silent.

I take a deep breath and let it out slowly before I answer. "I cannot promise anything when it comes to your protection. You are my priority and if someone is making you so afraid that you have a pistol for protection . . . Alyssa, I need to fix it by whatever means necessary."

She leans her forehead into me, and I give her the time to find the courage to speak again. I know whatever she is not wanting to tell me; it's for a good reason.

Just by the sheer fact the guy showed up here the way he did has put him on my shit list. Anything else is just a bonus.

"Okay," she finally huffs. "Haley hated him."

I nod but stay silent; I know mentioning Haley is hard enough for her.

"She always told me there was something about him that seemed off. He never wanted to come to family events. He was upset that I was in my own sister's wedding and had to walk down the aisle with another man. He started arguments over the smallest things."

Other than my thumb rubbing across her arm from my hold, I stay silent and take it all in.

"He had my nerves all out of whack. I never knew when the next argument would come. Either my hair was too done or my makeup. He always told me I was trying to impress others. Or lord forbid I went weeks without wanting to have sex. He swore he could get it from somewhere else if I didn't put out."

I know the moment she could tell my anger is boiling from my breathing when she turns her head to face me. When my eyes meet hers, a single tear slides down her face.

"Alyssa you are safe. I am not going to let him hurt you again," I assure her.

"That's not the worst of it, Collin." She turns her head, looking at the wall opposite of us.

"After Haley died, I became severely depressed. I was not myself. My twin, my best friend, and my person in life, left me."

By now a flood of tears are pouring down her face.

"And that's when his mental abuse turned physical." Her face turns to read my reaction, and I have to physically retrain myself in my seat.

"He forced sex on me, the bruises he put on my arm and ribs were getting harder and harder to cover up and came at times I least expected. He even went as far to tell me 'I don't want you but no one else can have you either.' He stalked me everywhere I went. Would sit outside my work and follow me home to make sure I was alone. He even went as far as to tell everyone around us I was a whore, and they should stay away from me."

She pauses and takes an even bigger breath, "What makes matters worse, I was engaged to him. So, I thought I was stuck in that hell for the rest of my life. Eventually, I got enough courage to break it off."

I brush the hair out of her face and wipe the tear that leaves her eye.

She continues, "When we broke off the engagement, I told him he could come get his things. He was so angry with me when he arrived, he forced me onto the bed, stripped my clothes, and pushed himself on me. Once he was done, his phone rang. It was his girlfriend—or a woman he was seeing. I am not even sure who she was; we hadn't been broken up for long. I had no idea there was anyone else. I could not even think about dating at the time. He literally covered my mouth while talking to her but inside me and proceeded to tell her he was on his way to her house, and he loved her. While he was laying over me."

Her whole body is shaking, and I take it upon myself to wrap her tighter in my arms and let her cry on my shoulder; this is not the time for me to blow up. It's the time for me to console her. I can deal with the son of bitch who did this to her later. As far as I am concerned, he has already marked his grave with me.

"Do you know how gross that makes you feel? Being the other girl. Being the girl that he just forced himself on while he talks to his other girl." She sobs into my chest.

"You were not the other girl. And I am so sorry he did that to you."

Her breathing slows. "I did care about him at one time. But he destroyed me. I was already mourning my sister's death. And his actions sent me right over the edge. I thought the only way out was death."

My nostrils flare: this prick almost took my girl from me before I ever met her.

Her head raises to look at me. "Want to know the day I had decided I was going to do it?"

I raise an eyebrow, "When?"

"A few hours before I met you. I had gone to get a bite to eat before I did it. My last meal."

My heart pounds in my chest faster than before. But this time it's not from anger; it's from something else. Something in my chest that feels like it's medicine to my soul. Maybe even a little bit of thankfulness, too.

I remember the day I met her like it was yesterday, though it was a little over two months ago. I was at Nana's, our family restaurant in Maple, getting lunch since I worked all morning at the farm. Alyssa had stepped inside looking for a seat.

The hostess at the front was on break and no one was covering while she was gone so I stepped in while I waited on my to-go boxes.

The moment I saw her, I knew I wanted to see her again. She was the most beautiful woman I had ever laid eyes on.

Before I knew it, I had talked her into getting a plate to go and bringing her back to the farm with me.

Here I am two months later, not a doubt in my mind that she is where I belong.

I brush the hair out of her face, tucking it behind her ear, and glide my finger over the tear that sat on her cheek. "In case no one has told you this, I am so proud of you. For not only getting away from him but also for still being here. You are the best thing that has ever happened to me and God as my witness, you will never fear for your safety again."

I don't give her time to respond before my lips crash into hers.

Chapter Five
Alyssa

Whatever weight I was carrying in my chest is gone the moment his lips touch mine. Nothing else in the world matters besides his touch on me.

Parting my mouth with his tongue, he invades me, rectifying every ounce of sadness I had before now.

Picking up my body, and straddling his lap, I sit down right on his bulge. This man can get a boner when I am around faster than I ever thought possible.

My arms wrap around his neck, pressing my breasts into his chest.

"You sure know how to make a girl forget all the negative things," I whisper, pulling away to catch my breath.

"You haven't seen nothing yet." He stands, with my legs wrapping around his torso and walking me down the hall into the bedroom.

"I want to remind you of something." Collin's soft but deep voice makes the hair on my arms stand up. I know that voice. It's his horny voice.

He lays me down on the bed and I bite my lip to keep from giggling.

"And what is that?"

He pulls his shirt off over his head, in the sexy way men do by pulling it up from the back and lifting it in one solid move. I think my inner thighs got even more wet by that movement alone.

He crawls between my legs on the bed, lifting them, and slowly takes my sleep shorts off, exposing my underwear. His fingers grab either side of the fabric keeping a boundary between my flesh and him.

Slowly, he slides them down my thigh and throws them over his head once he has them off me.

"I am going to remind you what it feels like to have a man worship you the right way." His head lowers between my legs, but his eyes stay on me. "Watch me," he orders. "I want your eyes on me when you come undone on my tongue."

Yep. I am a goner.

If there is anything Collin Mapleson does well, it is dirty talk.

His hands reach under me, holding me up slightly by my cheeks before his tongue swipes over my clit. I never knew it was possible to take your time and completely go insane all at once but that's what he does to me.

Collin's tongue penetrates me before his mouth sucks over my clit. Repeating the action a few times before he takes a finger and sticks it in while his tongue teases my swollen bundle of nerves.

"Let's see how many fingers I can get in," he winks at me.

My body instantly tenses as he sticks another one in. "That's a good girl. Stretching for me."

This man and his mouth. I may come right now from his words alone.

He pumps his fingers in and out of me a couple times before adding a third finger. It's tight at first but my body instantly opens for him like it is meant for him.

His eyes stay on me, but his tongue goes back to making erotic flicks over my clit and the movement alone makes my back arch and a moan escape me.

"That a girl. Talk to me," Collin purrs and I instantly feel satisfaction from his praises.

My greedy body starts wanting more and rides his fingers, chasing the orgasm I can feel building inside me. I believe he can sense it, too, because his eyes grow dark, and he sucks my clit, nipping it with his teeth, making my toes curl, and the feelings of euphoria rush over me.

I don't know if I am in heaven or hell but one thing I am sure of, I don't want to be anywhere else than with Collin Mapleson.

***

COLLIN

My phones alarm goes off at sunrise the next morning, jolting me out of my sleep. A little disoriented, I look around and realize quickly I am in Alyssa's bed.

Her naked body is wrapped up in the covers beside me, her hair draped down her back while her breathing is settled into an even rhythm.

"Hey, Pretty girl." I whisper raising my hand to her forehead to brush back some of her hair.

Her eyelids move before her body. A gentle smile spreads across her face. "Hey to you, Cowboy."

"Megan is going to be wondering where I have been. I need to get home and get my chores done." I explain but we both know I don't want to leave this bed any more than she does.

She sighs, "I need to meet her, Collin."

And I know she does. It has been so nice being in our own little cocoon lately. I don't want anything to mess it up.

"And you will." My voice is low. Maybe I am trying to assure her as much as I am myself.

"When?" she asks with a grin.

"I don't know yet," I tell her honestly.

She huffs, siting up, and climbing out of bed. Grabbing her house coat from the bathroom she eventually comes back into the room and says, "Okay then. Whenever you are ready, I am ready."

I reach out my hand for her and her eyebrow lifts.

"I don't trust you." She laughs.

"It's a deal; we have to shake on it," I nod at my hand.

Her body is tense as she makes her way to me. Slowly raising her hand, when it meets mine, I take the opportunity and pull her into me on the bed and pin her down.

"Collin!" she squeals.

Lowering my head, I kiss her neck, her chest, and back up to her lips.

"Say my name, Pretty girl. Just like you did last night." I wink.

She giggles and the sound does something to my chest. I could listen to her laugh and be happy all day long.

"Are you going to be here tonight?" she asks, and I can see the worry in her eyes. She is afraid that fucker will be back. And honestly, I fear the same.

What would he have done had I not been here last night? My nostrils flare just thinking about him busting the door down and hurting her.

"Collin?" her eyes search mine getting my attention.

"Yes, baby. I will be back tonight."

"What are you going to tell Megan?"

I shrug. "I am a grown man. She does not have to know everything about my life."

Finally jumping out of bed, we get ready for our day.

"Here," I say, walking into the kitchen while she fixes her morning coffee. It's not much but I want her to have something on her just in case.

"Collin . . ?" she sighs looking at the pistol I am handing her.

"I won't be able to be with you for most of the day. Take it with you just in case. I have Cade and the guys watching your place while I am not here. He told me a few minutes ago he would make sure a deputy sits out by the restaurant while you are there. It would give me peace of mind knowing you had something to protect yourself, too." I give her a reassuring grin. "Just in case."

And I mean it. *Every word.*

I have told Cade that she will be armed. I am not taking any chances with her safety. The son of a bitch hurt my girl and while I am around, I will be damned if he gets near her again.

"Thank you." She looks at me, a twinkle in her eye.

"For what?" I raise an eyebrow.

Protecting what's Mine

"For protecting me."

I lean in, giving her a soft kiss. "I always protect what is mine."

Chapter Six
Collin

The morning sun has risen above the mountains of the back pasture by the time I pull up at the barn for my day.

The dogs run off the porch to meet me, wagging their tails, and fighting for attention.

"Morning guys," I tell them with a laugh as I open the truck door.

Today is looking like it will be a beautiful day. All the buds on the trees and plants are starting to open up, and Grandmother's tulips she loved so much are opening by the front porch.

I am not sure what Megan has on her schedule today, but I do know there are horses to be ridden, hay to be delivered, and some fences to be mended.

Thankfully, it does not look like Megan is up yet or at least is not outside.

Hopefully I can make it look like I got in late and got up early.

I close my truck door slowly trying my best to keep the noise to a minimum without calling attention to myself.

Walking carefully to the barn my feet freeze in their place when I hear, "Where have you been?"

I knew this was too easy. I am shocked the little shit has not had a welfare check out on me by now if she knew I was gone.

"You know," I turn facing her with my best grin only a little brother could have, "The way you just said that reminds me of Mrs. Weasley in Harry Potter."

I walk up to the porch to stand at the bottom of the stairs to mock Megan, "No note. Beds empty. You could have died!" I clutch my chest on the last part.

She rolls her eyes biting back a laugh, "Where did you go?" She gestures to my truck, and I say the first thing that pops into my mind.

"To grab breakfast."

Her eyes narrow at me, "Where is mine?"

I turn, waving her off and give an evil chuckle, "Darling sister. I said I went to get ME breakfast. Not get US breakfast."

"Collin!" she yells jogging up to me by the time I reach the barn.

Molly's head pops out of her stall and her ears shoot forward noticing Megan. "Bite her Molly," I tell the beloved mare while I give her scratches on the head.

"I am going to ride the colts today," Megan informs me walking into the tack room.

"Roger that."

Honestly, I am glad she is here to ride the colts now. Our breeding program has been going well. Almost too well. And I am tired of being thrown off colts and dealing with their attitude. My body needs a break, or I am going to end up in a wheelchair before I am thirty.

"Heard anything from Nationals?" I ask her curiously. She has been working hard to earn a spot back and I hope she gets it.

"Nah. But they said it could be a month or so." Her voice echoes from the tack room.

I decide to leave it be and not push too hard. One thing I have learned about Megan, you cannot push, or she will pull. And by pull, I mean PULL YOUR ASS TO THE GROUND.

She comes out with a halter and lead rope, "What is your plan today?"

I gesture to the Ranger that sits in the hall of the barn. "I will fix those posts in the side pasture."

She nods, agreeing while she walks into one of the colt's stalls to saddle him up.

Protecting what's Mine

∗∗∗

It has been a ball-busting day. Meaning everything is hurting on my body while I have been mending these fences and all I want is to be balls deep in my girl.

Ding. Ding.

Speaking of my pretty girl.

I am on break. Thinking about you. Hope you are having a good day.

A fat grin runs across my face, and I slip the work gloves off my hands to reply to her text.

Be better if I was with you. :)

I lean up against the tailgate of the Ranger and wait for her response.

Three bubbles pop up and I feel anxious waiting to see what she says.

Don't make any plans later. I want to cook for you tonight.

I let out a soft laugh. This girl knows how to do a lot of things, but cooking is not one of them.

Will it be edible or burnt? I ask.

For a minute, I think she might block my number for that.

I will spit in it, too, just for that.

My cock twitches and my fingers fly over the keys with an instant reply.

I have something else you can spit on.

The three bubbles pop up and disappears three different times before her text finally delivers.

Collin Mapleson. Where did you get such a dirty mouth?

I reply, *you are the one whose mind is in the gutter. I was simply implying you could spit on my shirt later to get the dirt stains out.*

She knows me too well because my mind was not thinking about my fucking shirt.

I am full of shit, and she knows it.

Whatever you say. I am cooking tonight.

Before I have time to reply she shoots another text back.

Break's over. Got to get back on the floor. See you tonight, Cowboy.

I smile, leaning off the tailgate, tucking my phone back into my pocket, and grab my Gatorade from the inside of the Ranger, taking a big gulp of it.

I may stop and grab a pizza on my way to her place just in case.

Protecting what's Mine

She really cannot cook.

***

The parking lot of Nana's is nearly full when I pull in to grab a pizza. I called ahead and our head cook said he would get it ready for me.

Looking through my keys, I find the one for the back door and slip in that way, trying my best to avoid the dinner rush.

"Whew, I am shocked you had time to cook one up for me," I tell Danny, our head chef. He is a middle-aged man who Grandmother hired about twelve years ago. She taught him all her recipes and secrets to making them taste just like her cooking.

For that, I will be forever thankful.

Danny turns around and chuckles. "Anything for my favorite kiddos."

"You mean kiddo." I wink. "We all know I am the superior Mapleson."

He laughs but doesn't agree or disagree. Grabbing a to-go pizza box by the stove, he passes it to me. "Extra cheese like you like."

"Thank you, sir." I grin at him and put a twenty-dollar bill in his apron pocket.

"Collin, I get paid for cooking here," he laughs.

"You get paid for cooking for those people." I point out into the dining area. "But I should never expect you to drop what you are doing to cook for me. Especially during rush hours."

His grin turns prideful, "You remind me of your grandfather. Never lose that, son."

I fight back tears and nod. "Night, Danny."

Closing the door I came in from and locking it back, I wipe the tear I was fighting while inside.

That was the best compliment I could ever receive.

Fifteen minutes later, I am pulling my truck into a parking spot in front of her apartment complex, deciding it would be best to leave the pizza I picked up from Nana's in the passenger seat until I know it's safe to bring it in.

"I'll be back to get you in a few minutes." I tell the pizza box before shutting my door and putting my cowboy hat on top of my head. Normally, I would leave it in my truck but tonight I have other plans for it.

Knocking on her door, I hear someone say 'shit' on the other side and I chuckle. I am surprised the whole fire department is not out here yet.

"Hey!" the door flies open, and Alyssa is smiling—a stressed out smile—on the other end. I bite my tongue to keep from laughing because she looks like she has literally just walked out of a food fight war.

Her apron is full of flour, there is something dark on her cheeks, and her hair is in a tangled mess on top of her head, that I might add has flour in it too.

"You look . . .," I start, but she puts up a finger to stop me. "Don't you even say it."

She heads back into the kitchen quickly, and I shut the door behind me making sure to lock it. Cade and his guys have not seen Kyle since he was here the last time but that does not mean he's not still around.

Men like him have their ways of being hidden until they need to be seen.

"Ugh. It's burnt." Alyssa's voice sounds like she is about to cry as she pulls out a tray from the oven. When the smoke rolls out, the smoke detector goes off, startling us both.

"Pretty girl, let me fix it for you." I tell her walking up and closing the oven, taking the tray from her hands, and walking over to the smoke detector turning it off.

"The pizza is burnt." She is now fully crying. "I was trying to do something nice for you. And now we don't even have pizza to eat."

I smirk, grabbing her arms and pulling her into me. After a moment I assure her. "Yes, we do. Let me go back out to my truck."

Her head pops up. "Collin Mapleson. You had no faith in me to begin with, did you?"

"Of course I did. I just did not want to risk starving all night just in case." I wink.

Thankfully her tears are gone, and she giggles. "Well go get it, goofball. I am starving."

I salute her and walk back out to my truck to get our dinner that is not burnt.

Chapter Seven
Alyssa

I had this whole romantic evening planned. Collin works harder than anyone I have ever met, and he is exhausted when he gets off from the farm.

Somehow, he still takes the time to make meals for me; I wanted to do the same in return.

But he is right, I can't cook worth a shit. *It's the thought that counts right?*

Of course, he sweeps in like freaking Prince Charming and saves the day.

I have never had a man take care of me the way he does. He is always one step ahead of me and at first it made my brain misfire.

Coming from an abusive relationship with Kyle, I did not know that men like Collin even existed. Sure, I had seen my parents fall in love and my sister too. But I had always accepted that was not in the cards for me.

Until Collin Mapleson came along.

I mean sure, I thought I did love Kyle at one time; but love doesn't make you mistreat the person you are with.

On the day I was going to end it all; Collin came out of nowhere and since then he has not left my side. Where I am cautious and full of anxiety, he is the calm to my storm.

I look around my kitchen at the mess and feel exasperated.

All of this for a burnt pizza; *how Alyssa of me.*

The door opens and he walks in looking all handsome in his cowboy hat, boots and Wranglers, but it's the pizza in his hand that turns me on the most. I can smell it from here and from the sound my stomach just made, it approves too.

Collin sets the pizza on the table, opening the box and gesturing to it. "Sit and eat, you've had a busy day."

I laugh, "I can't eat until this mess is cleaned up." I point at the kitchen.

"I know," he tells me. "That's why I am going to clean it up and you are going to sit down, prop your feet up, and eat your dinner."

"No." I shake my head, "That is not fair. You need to eat too."

"And I will. Once I clean this mess up for you and I know your stomach is happy and fed." He walks over to me pressing a kiss to my forehead.

I stand up on my tip toes grabbing his cowboy hat off his head and putting it on mine. "You are every woman's dream, Collin Mapleson."

He smiles. "You know what it means when you take a cowboy hat off a cowboy and wear it don't you?"

I raise an eyebrow. "No?"

"It means you get to ride the cowboy." He winks and I can feel my core heat up from the look he gives me alone. Or maybe it's because he has brought us food. Or the fact that he is currently cleaning up the kitchen that holds the mess I made.

"How well you clean up my kitchen will determine how well you get ridden," I smirk.

Honestly, I am just joking at first, but by the way his nostrils flare when he looks at me, I think I may have just poked a bear I have not met before.

My stomach rumbles again so I obey and sit down, grabbing a piece of pizza from the box, and watch my handsome man clean up a mess he did not make.

Nobody pinch me if I am dreaming right now. I don't want to wake up. I want to sit right here with my feet elevated, stuffing my face, and watching his handsome butt in those Wranglers.

***

Collin

She watches me the entire time and I cannot help but smile.

A few months ago, I would have told all my buddies no woman would make me settle down. I was going to live my single cowboy life and be a bachelor for as long as I could.

Until I met Alyssa. The woman captivated me to the point I caught myself wanting to become *domesticated*.

Sure, our relationship is still new, but I find myself wanting to come home to her and not the farm.

The farm will always be my physical home, but slowly *she* is turning into the place that is my *home.*

She is the place that keeps me going, makes me want to be a better man, and make a life with.

I have not told her yet, but I am falling in love with this woman who snuck in without an invitation and has taken up residence.

I will gladly give her a key if she will just stay forever.

Throwing the towel I used to dry the dishes I washed over my shoulder, I walk over to the pizza box and grab a piece out, smiling when I see three missing pieces.

"Glad you left some for me." I joke.

She giggles. "Thought you might need your strength."

I raise an eyebrow. "Oh darling, it's you that needs her strength. I have plans for you tonight."

She raises an eyebrow. "Plans?"

I take a bite of my pizza, swallowing slowly, and grabbing the glass of sweet tea she fixed sitting by her and take a sip before I answer.

I have thought a lot about this and spent most of my time today on the farm researching. "Do you trust me?"

She nods but her eyes tell me otherwise.

"Alyssa, I need you to trust me. But all you have to say is no if it's a problem."

"I trust you, Collin." She whispers.

When we first had sex, I tried grabbing her throat because some girls like that and she freaked out on me. Of course, I stopped, and she ran off crying. She would not tell me why she reacted that way and I never pushed the issue.

I should have asked her before I did it but as bad of an excuse as it is; it was in the heat of the moment, and I got carried away.

Her reactions like that do not happen every time. I can still dirty talk her and it doesn't faze her; or like the other day, in the shower, she was okay because she initiated it.

It's when I try to be more physical, in a way of being kinky, it turns a switch on in her brain to run.

Now that I know about Kyle, it all makes sense; *she has PTSD.*

And who could blame her? The sick fuck that he is deserves a good beating to force anything on her or abuse her. Her mind is traumatized.

After she told me about his abuse, it all clicked in my head.

So, I have been Googling ways to help her. If I can show her how in control she can be in the bedroom, maybe it will help her heal her past trauma and feel confident again.

"I want you to know you will always be in control." I pause to read her eyes before I continue. "Have you ever looked into PTSD?"

She nods. "I have self-diagnosed myself."

I smile, "Well, at least you are aware. That is step one." I raise my hand and brush some hair out of her face, "I have researched ways to help you. Did you know certain things in the bedroom may help? Some therapists say things like feeling in control is a treatment some people use."

She nods. "I have read on them. I just did not know how to bring it up to you."

I grab her hand pulling her out of her chair and into me. "You can talk to me about anything, pretty girl. I am here to help. We will dodge these curveballs together."

I push her hair out of her face again as I look down at her. "Has he shown his face again since last night?"

She shakes her head, no. "I am hoping that means he is gone."

I nod but stay silent. A narcissist like him wouldn't leave that easy. But I don't tell her that.

Instead, I bend down, pressing my lips to her softly. Lowering casually, I wrap my arms under her ass and pick her up. She instinctively wraps her legs around my waist, and I lead us down the long hall into the bedroom.

"For this to work you have to communicate with me," I tell her easing her back down onto the mattress.

She sits up when I walk away to shut the bedroom door. "Don't be mad if I panic."

I graze my fingers over her already flushed cheek, leaving them still for a bit longer than I intended. "Pretty girl. You are in control in here. If you feel like you are going to panic, tell me and we will stop."

She grins. "What do you have planned?"

"You tell me. I want you to have the control." I wink.

My cowboy hat still sits beautifully on top of her head, and I hope she doesn't take it off while we do this.

"Get naked, Mr. Mapleson." She smiles so big her eyes twinkle. "I want you laying on the bed, fully ready for me."

"Yes ma'am." I salute her teasingly and she rolls her eyes playfully.

Backing up from the bed, my eyes stay locked on hers while I pull my shirt off, exposing my tired and blood pumped muscles from working all day.

Her greedy eyes sparkle watching me, making my dick throb in appreciation.

Reaching for my pants button next, I unbutton them slowly, pulling the zipper down before gliding my pants down my butt and thighs until they land on the floor.

"Wait." She tries her best to hide her smile by biting her lip. "Don't take the boxers off yet. Come lay down."

"Yes, Madame." I wink and she swats at me when I cross her to lay on the bed.

My cock feels like it's going to explode in my boxers as soon as she stands above me. She looks so beautiful, and right now I am seeing her truly for who she is.

A normally anxious and worried person who stands before me, carefree and swaying above me. A big smile on her face and sparkles in her eye. If I can find a way to bring that side of her back fully, I will one thousand percent believe I have found my purpose in life.

My smile must be evident since she asks, "Why are you so happy, Mr. Mapleson?"

I resist the urge to grab her and pull her down to me. "Seeing you happy makes me happy, pretty girl."

She must like that answer because she kneels in-between my legs and makes her way up to my face. "You make me happy."

Her lips crash onto mine and before I have a chance to, her tongue sweeps into my mouth, taking all the control from me.

Normally, control is where I thrive. It's what I like best. But this right here, her owning her own self and being confident might be my new favorite thing in the world.

My dick would agree, too.

Chapter Eight
Alyssa

Kyle would take from me without asking. He would use violence or force to get his way. Most of the time I would just lay there and take it because I knew there was no other way to stay away from his wrath and that was honestly worse than anything else.

Collin has always been careful with me in the bedroom—or shower.

I knew he always wanted more from me, but he would never tell me. Since the night I panicked when he put his hands around my throat and I ran out of the bedroom freaking out, he kept it very vanilla. But the way he would dirty talk to me, I knew he was interested in other things.

And I would love to experience those things with him.

I have no control over my *episodes.* Everything can start out fine and then suddenly, my mind thinks something seems too familiar and makes me go into fight or flight mode. A feeling that leaves me feeling sluggish for a few days afterwards.

It's almost like my mind tells me, "This seems too much like what happened before when you almost died. Let's stay far away from it."

And while I am thankful for it looking out for me, it's starting to get old.

I thought grieving my sister was going to be the worst trauma I could ever experience.

Until it wasn't.

Having control right now with Collin laying at my mercy is empowering to say the least. And it is freaking turning me on.

Holy cow, I can feel how wet I am from my underwear.

I break away from our kiss and slowly spread kisses along his neck, his chest, stomach, and stop right before I get to the good part.

"I think I am going to tease you for a while." I smirk when Collin's nostrils flare. He is turned on as much as I am.

I raised my shirt up over my head, exposing my breasts in my lacy black bra. Standing up, I move my hands to my shorts, unbuttoning and sliding them down my legs.

Slowly stepping out of them and throwing them off the bed. Collin's eyes never leave mine until they run down my body and stop right at my underwear.

"Oh, you like these?" I tease.

He purrs, "I like what they hide underneath."

"Oh." I bite my bottom lip. Lacing my fingers through the fabric of my panties, I pull them down slowly, exposing the area he was referring to.

"Better?" I ask.

He growls. "Be even better if you come sit on my face."

I shake my head, no. "I am in charge remember?"

His nostrils flare again, and I know for a fact I have him right where I want him.

I think of what to do next. This is all new to me but being in control has given me a whole other confidence I didn't know I had.

At least for the time being.

Unlatching my bra, I free my breasts and grab my nipple pinching hard until my eyes roll back, and I moan.

"Yes, pretty girl." Collin hums. "You look so beautiful."

His boxers seem like they hurt from how tight they look right now. I think about freeing him but stop myself when another thought crosses my mind.

Slowly gliding my hand that was pulling on my nipple down my stomach and over my wet flesh. My back arches when it glides over my clit. All this teasing has got me worked up as much as it has him.

My eyes lock on his, and I think for a moment he might leap from where he is laying.

"Watch, Cowboy. Don't move." I tell him before I slide a finger into my flesh and pump it in and out. The sound of my wetness takes over the room and Collin licks his lips.

"That a girl. Stretch yourself for me." Before I realize what I have done, another finger slides in.

"Oh my god," I moan. "Collin take your boxers off."

"Don't have to tell me twice," he says, making me giggle.

Removing my hand, I crawl over to him, sticking my fingers inside his mouth.

"Suck." I tell him and his eyes darken. "About damn time," he growls before licking and sucking my wetness from me.

Once he is done, I push him back down on the bed and straddle him, his tip hitting my wetness perfectly.

His eyes fall back, and he has to physically restrain himself from grabbing me, so he grabs the sheets.

I laugh. "Hold on cowboy. I am going to keep your hat on for the ride."

I slowly sit down on his shaft and feel it stretching me as it slides inside me.

"So much better than my fingers," I mumble in between my breaths.

Collin nods. "Ride me pretty girl."

And I do. I ride my beautiful cowboy until we both reach our climax and become one together. The only person I would want to try new experiences with.

Chapter Nine
Collin

It has been almost a full week since Megan has been home, and I know she needs to meet Alyssa. The girl I want to marry someday needs to meet my sister and I cannot keep putting it off.

Eventually, someone from town is going to tell her and she will be even more upset that I was not the one to do it.

Alyssa has been doing well with our "play time." At least, that is what we are calling it. Her PTSD episodes stem from feeling weak, not in control, and fear.

My hope is if we can keep doing things where she is in control, eventually, she will feel in control of her life again. The moment she puts the control back in my hands, will be the day I know this little experiment has worked.

It is finally the weekend, and I arrived at the farm this morning earlier than normal to get some work done because I have plans to take Alyssa to Hilltop tonight.

Maggie and Logan took Rhett to her dads for a few weeks. He doesn't live close by, and Maggie thought extra hands while she recovered from giving birth would be helpful.

Not that we couldn't help them, but the farm is a lot within itself to take care of.

Kyle really seems to be gone. And while I still have my guard up, it wouldn't hurt to let my girl have a fun night. She deserves it.

Plus, it will be a good excuse to get Megan out of the house to meet Alyssa, too. Maybe at least there she won't pitch a fit with a lot of people around.

Who am I kidding? It's Megan; she would pitch a fit to Jesus Christ if she was mad enough.

The evening sun will be setting soon and my chores for the day are finally coming to an end. I walk back through the barn one last time, making sure everyone has hay and water for the night and give Molly a scratch on the side of her neck while she has her head stuck out of her stall door.

"Keep everyone under control tonight, girl," I tell her.

Bending over the door, I double check the lock that keeps her stall door closed; she is a Houdini and likes to let herself out of her stall.

Soon as I flip the light off in the barn, my phone dings, alerting me of a text message.

Alyssa: I will meet you at Hilltop. Just got home and going to grab a quick shower.

I smile. I am beyond ready to see my girl. My fingers scan over the screen of my iPhone.

Be careful, pretty girl.

Looking down at my pants and boots making my way back to the farmhouse I realize I need a shower, too.

Megan doesn't know I am going out tonight and I figured it was best to wait to ask her to go with me until we were both done for the day.

Opening the screen door to the kitchen, I spot her instantly sitting at the kitchen table looking over paperwork for the farm, I assume. She looks exhausted and like she could use a break. I thank the gods above because she may not put up much of a fight to get out of here for a while.

Walking past her to the fridge, I get her attention. "Meg, want to go to Hilltop tonight?"

I don't look at her. Instead, I open the door of the refrigerator and take a water out.

"You mean to tell me that place is still busy?" She looks up from her papers.

I smirk, taking a sip of my water. "You know us small town folks. We don't like change much."

She grins, making the pit in my stomach settle. "Sure. When do you want to go?"

"Give me an hour or so to change. I smell like horse shit."

She nods, looking back down at the paper on the table as I rush upstairs to get ready.

Whew, that was easy enough. Now, I need the nerves in my stomach to stop fluttering.

***

If I had been thinking clearly, we would have taken Megan's truck tonight so I could let her leave in it while I rode back with Alyssa to her place.

But since I knew for a fact my sister and girlfriend were meeting for the first time tonight; my brain has been nonexistent.

Hilltop was always our favorite place as teenagers and young adults. It's the place we brought our cousin, Maggie, and where she met her now husband, Logan.

I still laugh about her pouring her beer all down his head that first night.

"Geez," Megan starts once she steps out of my truck onto the gravel parking lot of Hilltop. "I think this place has gotten busier since I left."

She follows me to the front door. "Yeah, we had some young new people show up looking for work. They all like hanging out here on the weekends and weekdays too."

I hold the front door open for her to walk on in. Soon as everyone sees her, they all rush over, hugging her. One thing about Maple; it's a small town with a lot of love from the local folk.

And the fact that our family was the founder of the town might have something to do with it too.

The whole town has watched us grow up, and now that our grandparents have passed on, it's our legacy to keep the town up and going.

I walk off soon as the crowd gathers around Meg. The main reason is because I don't want anyone to mention Alyssa to me in front of her.

The best thing for me to do is give her space to see everyone. I'll catch up with her later.

"Hey man." Cade gets my attention from the pool table, and I nod walking over to him and some of our other friends.

"Hey brother." I nudge him as I walk by and find a stool to sit on to watch the pool game.

Cade has been one of my best friends since high school. While he is a local police officer now, he is also a volunteer fireman too. One of the best humans I know, with a heart of gold.

He lowers the stick down to hit the cue ball to the solid red on the far corner pocket. It sinks and he stands confidently, going to his next shot.

"I think he is hustling me," Brandon, another friend of ours says.

I chuckle. "Not a cop. He would do no such thing."

They all chuckle around us.

"I know you are glad Meg is home." Cade starts lining up for another shot. "Has she met Alyssa yet?"

All the guys turn to me, curious for my answer too.

I shake my head. "They are meeting tonight."

Cade whistles. "Remind me to stand near the exit in case I need to leave when things get messy. Remember, I am off duty tonight."

I smirk. "That's why I wanted to do it here. She won't cause a scene here."

All the guy's stare at me like I have lost my mind.

"Collin. You are a dumbass if you really think that." Cade says pointily.

I know he is right, but I had to try it.

I love my sister with all my heart, but giving up her control of me is just not something she does well.

I laugh internally at the thought: *I am trying to teach one how to be in more control and one I wish would give up some of her control. The fucking irony.*

"Speaking of Megan," Cade points over to the bar. "Might want to go see what that is about."

I turn my stool around to see my sister toe-to-toe with a guy who looks like an ex-convict.

I sigh. "So much for wanting her to be calm."

Jumping off the bar stool, I hurry over where they stand, arriving just in time for her finger pointing into the man's chest and her voice saying, "You will not talk to me that way."

"Everything okay over here?" I can feel my buddies behind me. Good thing too, because with Megan, I may just need back up.

Not for the guy. It's not him I am worried I will need backup for.

"It's fine, Collin." She waves me off. "Mr.— I'm sorry. I didn't get your name."

She looks at him for an answer.

"Derek." The mystery guy says.

"Mr. Firefighter Derek was just going to leave me the hell alone before I kick his ass."

"Derek Murphy?" I ask.

"Collin, Go Away," my annoyed sister tells me.

But I ignore her. Instead, I reach out my hand to the man that deserves it. "You are the one who saved our barn a few weeks ago?"

Derek nods but his gaze does not leave Megan's.

"What happened to our barn?" Megan's eyes are beholding me with anger.

Derek finally turns his eyes to mine and shakes my hand.

I sigh; this is not how I wanted her to hear about this either.

Hay is tricky. Sometimes it can go through heat if it's hot outside. We had an unusual hot day after rain the day before. It was so humid out too.

A few weeks ago, hay caught fire in our barn. Whoever bailed the round bails must have rolled them wet and we weren't made aware.

Instead of putting them in our other barn, we stored them in the hay loft in the barn we keep the horses. The loft is not ventilated well and caught on fire; it was almost catastrophic.

"We didn't want to worry you, Meg." I run my hands through my hair. "But our hay loft caught on fire a few weeks ago. Derek and his crew were first on scene. Logan and I couldn't put it out fast enough ourselves." I pause, not wanting to tell her the next part. "Derek saved Molly. A bale of hay fell through the loft right into her stall. He jumped in after her and got her out safely. We put new wood up before you got home so you wouldn't ask questions. We knew if you had known about it you would have dropped out of the circuit and came home."

My nervous system is already on defense. She could react a thousand different ways right now.

What she does shocks me. Taking a deep breath she turns to Derek. "Thank you for saving my old girl, but you are still on my shit list."

"That's Megan's way of giving a compliment." I assure Derek while letting a breath of air out of my lungs too.

In a world where there is a Megan Mapleson, this was the best way that scenario could have gone down.

"No, it's my way of being thankful for him saving the horse that means a lot to me; but I still don't consider him a friend."

We better stop now before she gets more upset and causes a brawl.

"Let me guess, you are going to be my new boss?"

For fuck's sake.

I have been so wrapped up in being with Alyssa, I forgot we had hired new help while Maggie and Logan were gone visiting her dad with Rhett.

"What the hell is he talking about?" Megan snaps at me.

Here we go.

I want to be anywhere else right now.

"A few weeks ago, before you came home, Maggie knew she and Logan would be gone for a while visiting her dad. So, we decided it was a good idea to hire some seasonal help."

I grin at her to try to soften the situation.

She turns towards the bar and drops her head dramatically.

"Yes. Unfortunately, I am your new boss," she tells him.

"When is it okay for me to move in?" Derek asks and I think I could strangle him.

Just shut your fucking mouth, dude.

I sigh, "You can move in tomorrow morning."

Before I know she's near me, Megan has grabbed me by the shirt, pulling me into her. "Move in where?" she exclaims.

"The house?" I give her a nervous grin.

If her eyes could kill, I would be a goner.

She mumbles something I cannot hear to Derek before storming off toward the bathroom.

"Is she always like this?" Derek asks me. He looks a little frightened. Or hot and bothered. I cannot seem to pinpoint which.

I pat him on the back, "You have no idea what fun you are in for."

Chapter Ten
Alyssa

I lost track of time trying to decide what to wear tonight. After standing in front of my closet for twenty minutes, I decided on a pair of skinny jeans, a strapless crop top, paired with a sheer blouse over the top.

I would be lying if I said I was not nervous – but I am trying my best to stay positive. Megan means a lot to Collin, and I want her to respect me too. One day, I hope we can be great friends.

I turn my blinker on to pull into Hilltop nearly thirty minutes past time that I told Collin I would be here.

Oops.

Grabbing my phone from the cup holder, I decide to leave my purse in the car and pocket a few twenties, just in case.

Collin normally pays for everything, but I never want to assume that he would. I am a big girl who can pay for her own things.

I will say, it is nice having a man in my life who is a gentleman in that way. Kyle was never that way – I mean of course. He was abusive but he never did the small gentleman things out in public either. I don't think I have ever seen him open my door, carry my bags, or pay for meals.

If I had my purse with me, he assumed I was paying for the both of us. And while I gladly did, that should have been my first red flag.

My phone dings in my hand before I open the door.

We miss you. Call us sometime. Cannot wait to meet Collin. He sounds like a wonderful man.

I smile. My mother and I have always been close.

Correction, my mother, Haley and I were always close. But when Haley died, my mother lost a part of her heart too. Just like I did. She grieved, and sometimes, I think I was too much of a reminder for her—and my father.

So, while I call them occasionally, I don't come around often. They do know about Collin, and I hope they get to meet him soon. A part of me feels guilty that I wanted to end my life and make them suffer again.

Another part of me wonders if they knew they were contributing to my grief too.

While I am not taking away from their own grief, I needed them too. And when they could not even look at me without crying or walking away—it wounded me.

I had no one in my corner anymore when I needed someone the most.

Since meeting Collin, I know how detrimental the decision to end my life would have been to those around me and what it would have cost.

And all the life I would have missed; like meeting the man of my dreams.

Meeting one of my good friends at my job.

And enjoying simple things like smiling again.

Collin likes to tell me, "Keep dodging those curveballs."

Apparently, that was something his grandmother always said to him and his sister. I find myself repeating the words a lot. Like when I am having a bad day at work, running into a psycho abusive ex, or meeting my maybe future sister-in-law.

I want nothing more than for Megan to like me.

To have a friendship with her would mean so much to me. I long for the friendship I used to have with my sister. And I love how close Collin and Megan are. I don't ever want to take her brother from her, and I hope she knows that.

Miss you guys too. Actually, about to go out on a date with Collin. Meeting his sister. Love you guys. I will call you sometime tomorrow.

A text comes back almost immediately.

Things must be getting serious. Love you too, sweetie.

I smile. I guess things are getting serious. I hadn't really thought about it like that. But over the last few months this cowboy has become my safe space, and I want whatever the future brings for us.

Grabbing my door handle, I step out, my short boots hitting the gravel parking lot. I admire how crowded it is making my way to the front door.

Lexie, my coworker and slowly becoming good friend, sees me soon as I step inside. She runs up and hugs me, her brunette hair hanging low on her back and green eyes sparkle with happiness.

"Girl, I have been waiting for you!" I look at her confused and then remember I told her earlier at work I would be at Hilltop tonight, and she could meet me here. She is new to town, and I figured it would be good for her to meet some new people: aka Collin's friends.

"Shit I forgot you were coming." I tell her with a laugh.

She grins. "Honestly, I am glad you even remembered to come. You have been so nervous about meeting Collin's sister tonight."

I look around. "Have you seen him?"

"Yeah, he's by the bar talking to his buddies." She points and my nerves instantly melt.

"Come on. I will introduce you to everyone." I grab her hand and lead her with me. "By the way," I start looking down at her outfit. She is dressed in ripped skinny jeans and a halter top with boots. "You look hot tonight."

She smiles, "So do you. Meow!"

We giggle as we continue our way through the crowd.

"Hey, handsome." I lean into Collin from behind and he spins around, grabbing me by the waist.

My eyes roam to the guys around us to introduce Lexi, but before I can say a word, my eyes collide with someone it shouldn't.

My sister's husband.

Or is he technically ex-husband now? What do you even call them? A Widower?

By the look on his face, he was not prepared to see me either.

I give him a soft grin, but his body looks like it needs to be anywhere else but here.

I hated him for so long. I convinced myself that the house fire she died in was his fault.

If he had not been stupid enough to leave a napkin next to a burning stove, my sister and unborn nephew would still be alive.

I cried and screamed and punched him in the chest at the hospital when the doctor came in to confirm our worst nightmare.

Derek left us after that. My father and he got in the biggest fight.

But he just up and left. No calls, no text. He kept us all from her graveside for so long. It was a nightmare.

I hated him so much. But one day I realized something else – he was grieving harder than any of us.

So over time, I realized accidents happen.

Derek would not have hurt my sister or nephew for anything in the world. He was sleep deprived and made a mistake. So unbeknownst to him, I forgave him.

That part I have never told him.

Because just like my mother and father, I know I remind him of Haley.

One of the curses of being a twin.

Collin and Derek mumble a few words to one another and then Derek takes off out the building.

Part of me wanted to go after him but I don't want Collin to get the wrong idea.

Derek is not my responsibility anymore.

He is fighting demons I don't know how to help him with. He is going to have to help himself first.

"I guess Megan left." Collin says looking around.

"All those nerves for nothing." Lexi pats my back, and I roll my eyes at her.

"Lexi this is the boys. You already know Collin." I smile back at my beautiful guy.

Cade, Collin's good friend, steps into Lexi, offering his hand to her. "Pleasure to meet you, Ma'am."

She raises an eyebrow. "Ma'am? What? Do I look like an old woman to you?"

"Oh great. You brought a live one." He winks at me.

"And I can kick your ass like one, too." She steps into him.

The tension between these two you could cut with a knife.

"Before you two start fucking in the bathroom, how about let's get these ladies some drinks." Collin chimes in and Lexie's face flushes.

"Better yet. Let me get the two beautiful ladies a drink." The voice alone makes all the hair on my body stand at attention.

Kyle.

He is standing behind the bar with a shit eating grin spread over his face.

Collin snakes a protective hand around my waist. "You need to leave this town."

Kyle leans across the bar on his elbows. "Let's get one thing clear, Cowboy. You don't call the shots around here. I do."

"No actually. I do," Cade says stepping beside Collin flashing his badge. Kyle backs down and puts his hands up. "No trouble, brother."

"I'll be the judge of that," Cade says.

Lexie grabs my hand, squeezing it for comfort.

"Kyle." I whisper. "Please just leave. I don't owe you anything."

He chuckles. The same sound he would make before he hit me or worse. It makes my heart rate spike. "Alyssa. You owe me forgiveness."

Collin snarls. "She does not owe you a damn thing."

"We will see about that." Kyle laughs. He walks backwards through the door behind the bar disappearing out of sight.

"Can you arrest him?" I ask Cade.

"Nope. He did not do anything wrong legally. And the fucker knows that." Cade growls.

Collin and Cade turn to me. "Have you ever shot a gun before?" Cade asks.

I shake my head, no. "I have one, but I have never used it."

Cade looks at Collin. "The best advice I can give you is to give her shooting lessons soon as you can."

Cade turns to me. "If he steps foot inside your property, you give him one warning and if he still comes inside to harm you, pull the trigger. I'll deal with the legalities."

I nod, grabbing on to Collin's shoulder.

"So much for a fun night out."

Chapter Eleven
Collin

I refuse to let Alyssa out of my sight the rest of the night. After Kyle showed his face, her nerves were on high alert, and I figured it would be best to get her back home.

"Lexie needs a ride home." Alyssa tells me when I ask if she is ready to go.

Her friend has had a few drinks at this point, and she absolutely should not be driving home tonight.

"Cade." I get my friends attention.

"Don't worry man. I already had planned to make sure she gets home safe." I raise an eyebrow, and he chuckles.

"Keep him in line, Alyssa," Cade tells my girl, giving her a hug as we tell them bye.

She walks over to Lexie, whispering something in her ear before making her way back to me.

"We have some pretty cool friends." She smiles at me. "I hate Megan didn't stay."

A part of me is glad she didn't stay but the other part of me wishes she had. By now, they would have met, and I would know how this would all play out.

"We will just have to try it again." I wink at her.

"Speaking of trying again," Alyssa smirks, walking out the front door with me, "Can we try again like we did the other night?" Her cheeks flush pink.

She is cute when she is embarrassed. "Whatever you want, Madame," I tease, and she slaps my shoulder.

Stopping on the other side of my truck, I am reminded that she drove here alone. Looking around, it's well past dark and I do not feel safe letting her drive back alone knowing that bastard is around.

But I will need my truck to get to the farm in the morning. Derek is showing up tomorrow and Megan has already shown her uncertainty.

"I will follow you home pretty girl," I tell her with a sigh. "I will need my truck to go to the farm tomorrow. Wrapping my arm around her waist, I see the uneasiness in her eyes. She's afraid he is watching her, too.

Lowering my lips to hers softly, I leave them there for a moment before pulling away. "You pull out first. I will follow behind you. I promise no one else will get behind you besides me."

She smiles, "I don't know what I would do without you Collin Mapleson."

"Let's not ever find out." I tell her, slapping her ass gently when she turns around walking to her car. I wait until she gets inside and her door shuts before I climb in my truck.

I made my girl a promise; I will follow behind her, stand behind her, and protect her always.

She has strength within her I am not even sure she knows she has . . . yet. But for now, I will make sure she feels comfortable and confident.

***

"Tell me about the farm." Her head lays over on my shoulder.

We have not been back at her place for more than an hour, and both decided to change into some comfortable pj's and lay on the couch for a while watching her favorite show, *Grey's Anatomy*, before retreating to the bedroom.

"What do you want to know?"

"I don't know. I just think it's cool that your grandparents built all of that for you, Megan, and Maggie."

I have told her about my grandparents on more than one occasion.

Their love is something I always thought fairy tales were made of. From my grandmother being a coal miner's daughter and meeting my grandfather, him going off to the war. They told us stories about a time my grandmother thought my grandfather was not going to come back home. She had to navigate raising their kids on her own.

Then my parents died, leaving Megan and I orphaned. My grandparents never doubted the decision to take us in and raise us.

They are all I have known growing up since our parents died when I was so young.

When Maggie came along, she was the missing piece to the puzzle we did not know we were missing.

We three got to witness our grandparents leaving this earth together and since then, we vowed to keep their legacy alive: the farm.

"Other than being with you, it's my favorite place." I give her my God's honest truth. It's my own piece of heaven and if she is up for it; I would love for her to make it her heaven, too.

"I have always loved horses," she starts. "I just never had any friends who owned them. Living in the city, you don't get livestock around a lot."

"Well, I know the perfect place for you to ride a horse." I grab her waist, lifting her up and over to straddle me. "Or a cowboy."

She rolls her eyes, but I know she feels my bulge under her by the smirk on her face.

"Tell me, Mr. Mapleson," she grinds herself over me making blood rush to my cock. Thank God I am sitting down, or I might just faint from the lack of blood in my head. "What dirty thoughts are you having right now?"

The question caught me off guard. My brain misfires for a minute because it's unlike my pretty girl to be so forward with her words in this situation. Gathering my bearings, I reach my hands to the hem of her shirt and raise it over her head.

Her breasts are free under it, and I silently thank the universe for that.

"I want to take your nipples in my mouth and suck on them while you play with yourself." My mouth goes dry watching her perky nips harden with my words.

"You have permission." She doesn't have to tell me twice. Dipping down, I grab the left nipple into my mouth, sucking while letting my teeth make tiny playful bites.

Alyssa's head rolls back at the sensation. I release her breast for a moment, allowing her to stand up to pull her pajama shorts down. To my surprise, she is not wearing panties either.

"Dear Lord woman, I think you want me to faint," I tease.

She giggles. "Someone needs to learn to control himself."

I grab her right nipple into my mouth, and she straddles me again, but this time allows enough room between me and her for her hand. The little tease knows exactly what she is doing.

Her hand grazes over my cock who is begging to be set free. It jerks and I think the image in front of me alone could make me lose control.

She runs her hands over her wetness; the sound lets me know how turned on my girl is. She is the one in control, until she asks me to be, but part of me does hope I get to slide my dick into that beautiful wet cunt tonight.

I know the moment she slips two fingers inside herself because she moans in appreciation.

"Collin." She moans.

"Yes, pretty girl."

"Will you put a finger in with mine?"

This girl is determined to get me to explode in my boxers.

"Yes ma'am." Lowering my hand to her, she pulls her hands out and I place mine to the back of hers. Allowing one finger to sit behind the two she has been using and letting her guide me inside with her.

"Oh my god." She moans. Her head falling back as our fingers stretch her together.

"I love how confident you are becoming." I tell her and it's the truth.

That fucker Kyle took her confidence away and I am slowly watching it come back.

"I need you," she whispers leaning into my ear.

"You got me," I assure her.

"No, Collin. I need you. Free your big cock."

Our fingers remove in rapid speed, and she stands above me, allowing me room to discard my boxers. My length stands to attention, ready for her warmth. She eases herself down, rubbing her wetness onto my head, before fulling submerging me inside her.

Our breath hitches together for a moment to get used to the sensation.

Alyssa stands slightly but sits back down quickly.

"Hold on cowboy," she winks.

And that is all I can do; hold on. My pretty girl rides me, her wetness sounding above our moaning, and it doesn't take long before we are both falling apart around one another in surrender. Her orgasm milks my own.

"You are something else," I tell her before planting a big kiss to her lips, my tongue sweeping in, parting hers, and making her moan into my mouth.

My dick goes hard again inside her.

Alyssa's eyes widen. "Round 2?"

***

The light shining in from the bedroom window makes me jolt awake, waking Alyssa in the process.

"Shit. I never set an alarm." I am frantic trying to find my pants and boxers.

Megan is going to kill me. Derek was starting his job on the farm this morning. For all I know, she's unalive him by now.

"Where is my phone?" I look around knowing good and damn well I have missed calls from an angry five-foot six woman who will not let me hear the end of this.

Alyssa grabs the covers, pulling them up around her, giggling at me while I panic.

"Thanks for the support." I wink at her.

She grins, "You are normally so calm and collected. This is a new side of you."

Finding my jeans, I pull them up and a t-shirt from the bag I keep here over my head. Walking to the edge of the mattress, I yank the covers back, exposing the most beautiful naked body of the woman I am falling in love with, and grab her feet, pulling her to me.

She squeals playfully. "You are staying here today?"

She nods, "Yes. I am off. Going to rest and clean up some. You wore me out last night."

I lean in, kissing her cheek, "It's you who wore me out."

She runs a hand over my neck. "Oops."

"There is a hickey on my neck isn't there?" I sigh.

"Sorry," she laughs.

"That's okay. I will just put one on you later."

As much as I hate to leave her right now, I don't have much choice. Bending down I kiss her deeply, leaving us both breathless.

"Don't be getting any prettier while I am gone." I whisper in her ear before slipping out of the bedroom, thankfully finding my phone on the kitchen counter and sighing heavily when I notice an abundance of missed calls from my sister.

Chapter Twelve
Collin

The smell of the to-go plates from Nana's roams throughout the interior of my truck. Our grandmother's restaurant has always been a comfort for us Mapleson kiddos and normally, our lunches come from there.

The fastest way to my sister's heart is food from Nana's. Call it cheating or not playing fair all you want, but I will not show up late empty handed if she has already—possibly—killed our new farm help.

Megan and Maggie own the restaurant now since it was left to them. I never had much to do with it, so it didn't come as a shock that it was left to the two girls.

Of course, I get my own cut of the profit but not as big as theirs. Most of my money comes from the farm itself and I would not have it any other way. The farm is where I thrive.

Turning on the driveway, the big **MAGNOLIA FARM** sign comes into view, making me smile. This farm is named after our cousin Maggie. Though we didn't know she was our cousin at first; honestly, when I met her, it was a rough start.

I walked in on her in the shower one time. To be fair, I didn't do it on purpose; I just really had to shit, and I mean, who forgets to lock the damn door?

This farm though, has taught us three some of the biggest lessons: Family first.

But my heart constricts a little at the thought of family. Slowly, but surely, Alyssa is becoming a part of my family too. And one day, if not already, she will come before my own family when, or if, we make our own.

I just hope Megan can let go enough to allow it to be a smooth transition.

A truck I don't recognize comes into sight as I drive closer to the farmhouse. Letting out a deep breath, I am thankful my sister has not killed the help . . . yet.

Who am I kidding? He could be laying in the hall of the barn or in the pond across the pasture. She is crazy enough to do it for sure.

Opening the door and grabbing the to-go plates, I make my way to the barn.

Reaching the door, I hear the two of them having a heated conversation. "Lunch is here!" I yell, making Megan jump and Derek chuckle.

"What the actual hell?! I have been calling you!" she puts her hands on her hips.

"Sorry. I got held up, but I brought us some lunch." I hold up the bag of lunch hoping it wins her over.

Shit. I forgot about the hickey on my neck. Turning quickly so she doesn't see it, I give her a big smile.

Too late. She knows something is up because when she steps into me, pulling my chin, she gasps. "COLLIN JEFFREY MAPLESON! I know that is not a hickey on your neck!"

I pull away quickly from her, trying to defuse the situation before it gets worse.

"Explain yourself!" she yells.

I try to think of a response fast. This is not the way I wanted her finding out about Alyssa. "Uh, there was a girl at the bar last night."

"Did you know about this, too? Why he was not here? And you didn't tell me?" she snarls at Derek.

Sorry dude, but it's every man for himself.

Derek throws his hands up in surrender.

"So, Collin, what did you bring us to eat?"

I smile. I might actually like having him here for backup.

"Lunch from Nana's." I wink at my sister.

I know I got her when she rolls her eyes, walking away from us and back to the house so we can eat.

"So, was it the blonde or the brunette?" Derek asks me.

Megan stops abruptly and turns to face us. "You both do me a favor and keep the pussy talk to yourself and away from me."

I nod, bending to kiss her on the cheek, and walk past her into the house. Thankful for the time being she has calmed down enough not to have a full-on manic episode on me over a hickey.

***

After lunch, Megan left Derek and me to ourselves. Honestly, I think it's for her sanity more than ours.

She took her plate from Nana's and left us alone in the kitchen, clearly not wanting to be around us in the slightest.

"Dude, you are killing me." Derek says, throwing a hay bale from the trailer into the hay loft. Farm work is making him look like an out of shape little girl.

I laugh, "Thought you ran into burning buildings and were a medic? Are you not supposed to be in shape?"

He picks up another bale and throws it with a huff. "I never said I was in shape. But apparently you need to be more than in shape to do this stuff every day."

"You haven't even seen the best part yet." I let him throw the last bale before I gesture to the Red Ranger sitting in the hall of the barn.

"Meg said there is a fence that needs to be repaired in the back side of the pasture. Might as well teach you while it is still daylight."

Derek grabs his bottle of water sitting on the back of the trailer the hay bales were on and chugs it. "Let's get this shit over with."

I jog into the tack room to grab the keys for the Ranger and slide in the driver's seat while Derek dips into the passenger side.

Turning the key, the engine roars, allowing us to drive off into the pasture of the most magical place I know: **Magnolia Farm.**

When I was a young kid, the farm felt like it was the whole world. The barn felt gigantic, and the animals felt like monsters coming to attack me.

But as I grew up, I learned this place is where all the worry that the world gives me gets taken away. It's the place where the animals have become some of my best friends.

I have watched seasons come and go. Life has been lost here but life has been gained as well.

"Is your sister always so cranky?"

I giggle at his question. I have noticed the tension between my sister and Derek. I also notice his body movement when she is around. If I did not know better, I would say Derek has a thing for my sister.

I smirk. "She is not so bad when you get to know her. She is just a believer in tough love. In her eyes, if you are easy to run off, you are not worth putting the time and effort into."

I pause, bracing myself, and Derek does too, as we cross the big creek on the back part of the pasture. Water splashes on both sides as we cross the deeper part onto the other side.

"I see the way you look at her man. Tread lightly. She is not some girl you get into bed with and then shove her out. It takes a lot to get her heart, but once you have it, you have it for life. Trust and words mean a lot to her. She watched our grandparents go through so much, and they were holding hands in the end. That is the kind of love she wants and deserves."

The tone in my voice on that last line even surprised myself.

"I do not look at her any type of way," he tells me.

I chuckle, "Whatever you say man. Just tread lightly."

My eyes scan the fence line as we ride through the pasture, and I quickly notice the fence Megan was talking about. A new line of barbed wire and posts need to be added. It looks like deer have been crossing here and over time, it has worn the post out and maybe some have been caught up in the wire pulling it down.

Stopping near the post but giving us enough room to move around it, I cut the Ranger off, place my phone in the cup holder, and jump out, grabbing my gloves and pulling them on.

"Come hold this post for me," I tell Derek, pulling the new post from the back of the tailgate. He makes his way around to me, pulling work gloves on over his hands.

I remove the old post and put the new one where I need it to be before Derek grabs it, holding it in place for me.

"I never thought I'd be working on a farm someday," he mumbles.

I pull the wire around the new post tightly. "Never thought I would meet someone who could rival my sister... or tries to." I look at him with a fat grin.

"I do not rival her." He rolls his eyes.

"Whatever you say man. All I know is no one questions her or tries to defy her. For some reason, you get under her skin easier than I do and that says a lot."

I lift my hand to hammer in some nails around the wire and post.

"So, what about that hickey?" Derek's question catches me off guard.

I grin, "I am not sure what you are talking about." I pull the barbed wire tighter around the lower part and hammer in the nails to keep it in place.

"Was it the blonde?"

I smirk up at him. "Do you know her?"

He shakes his head no before I go on. I don't want to tell him everything about Alyssa. That is her business and no one else's so I keep it as short and vague as I can. "Man, she is the most genuine, laid-back girl I have ever met. She has been hurt bad in the past. Said her family has been through a tragedy and she is just now getting back into the dating world. Though she says she has an ex that won't leave her alone."

I pause, taking a deep breath before saying this next part. "Don't tell my sister, but I have been staying with her some because she does not feel safe at night. He has tried to break in a time or two." My nostrils flare and I take another breath to calm down. "Why she chose me, I will never know. But you best damn well know I am going to do whatever I can to make her happy."

I go back to hammering the fence post with a grin on my face. Finally, the barbed wire looks like it will hold the post, and we can head back to the house – more importantly, I can head back to my girl.

Derek's head snaps to the side when a branch breaks near us. I look up too, my eyes widening when I realize what is starring back at us.

"Do you see it?" Derek whispers.

"Shit. My gun is in my truck back at the barn." My voice is muffled, trying to keep it low. The eyes of a bobcat is slowly moving towards us.

"Think we can make it?" Derek asks.

"I am not going down without a fight." Unfortunately, Derek is closer to the Ranger and the one who is more likely to make it out before me. He is also the one with the medical training if something were to happen.

"Derek, whatever happens, get to Megan," I mumble.

My heart rate speeds up, thinking about Alyssa, wishing I was with her, wishing and hoping I get to see her face, kiss her lips, and tell her I love her. I need to tell her I love her before I die. *Don't die.*

"On 3 . . .," I start.

"One," Derek says.

"Two," I whisper.

"Three!!" we say in unison.

I am only an inch from the Ranger when I feel it grab me. The claws ripping into my flesh. The pain radiating so bad I think I might die.

I scream out in fear and pain. Vaguely, I hear Derek screaming at the bobcat, and the claws I was feeling disappear.

"Call Megan!!" I scream before the world goes black.

Chapter Thirteen
Alyssa

My hips are swaying to the beat of Shania Twain's *Honey I'm Home* while dusting the tables in the living room.

Since Collin left this morning, I have gotten a lot done around the house I have been neglecting.

I've cleaned out my closet and made room for his things if he wants to bring some clothes over and a side of the vanity sink for him too.

The front door has been locked all day and, honestly, I am nervous to step out of it alone. Kyle is still around, and I would be lying if I said I was not scared of him.

When his hands did more than just bruise your body—but your soul too—that is often trauma that gets overlooked.

I moved to this apartment about a month before I met Collin. My family is from the city, which is not too far from here. I moved out of my parents' house and decided a place close, but my own, would be better. So, I decided on Cedarville.

Though it is more expensive than I originally wanted, I got a waitressing job at

Patsy's in town near the hospital and have made it work on my own.

Collin texted me after lunch earlier and told me he would bring supper with him when he headed home tonight.

Home. My heart swells with the words each time I look at it.

When I met this cowboy of mine, he was a stranger. Someone who just happened to run into a girl who was low on life and didn't want to live it anymore.

But since that day, he has given me a reason to keep living. He has given me a desire to get up every morning. He is the last thing I think about when I lay down at night and the first thing I think about when I wake up.

Sure, I still have shit to work through, but just having Collin Mapleson here with me makes it easier.

Setting down the duster on the kitchen table, I open the fridge and grab the tea pitcher, placing it on the kitchen counter. Reaching for a glass out of the cabinet, I fill it up with tea and put the pitcher back in the fridge. The first cold sip didn't make it down my throat before my phone dings alerting me of a text message.

I sit the glass down and walk over, gabbing my phone with a smile anticipating the dirty text I am sure Collin has sent me.

But my heart falls to my feet when it's a number that I thought I blocked months ago.

It's Collin. He was attacked by a bobcat on the farm. They have him in emergency surgery. It's bad. We are at Grace Memorial.

I have to catch myself before my knees hit the floor and with shaky hands I type back:

On my way.

Grabbing my keys off the counter and my purse off the couch, I don't even think about the psycho on the loose. I run out the door to my car.

Please let me get to tell him that I love him.

No God. Not again. I repeat to myself as I pull out on the main road.

I have not been inside Grace Memorial since Haley died. And I told myself I would never step foot back inside there.

Until the man I love needs me.

No amount of worry, fear, or anxiety could stop me from getting to him.

Hang on, Cowboy. Please hang on for me.

***

This hospital is the place my worst nightmare happened. I lost my best friend and sister.

Well, I know she was gone before she arrived but here is where it became real. It is the place I watched my mother hit and slap Derek, where my fist pounded his chest, and my father yelled at him, tears streaming down his face.

It is where I fell to my knees and screamed as I held my chest.

A part of me died with her that day – I could physically feel it.

And even though they say time heals all wounds, I call bullshit. Because as I stand in front of the doors that lead inside, my fight or flight wants to take over.

I hear the screams, the doctors telling us 'She is gone', and I feel the tears I shed.

That day I lost a piece of me, and now standing here not knowing what waits for me on the other side, *I am afraid.*

I am afraid if I lose another piece of myself, I may not come back from this again.

But if I had to walk through the deepest darkest places in hell for Collin, I would. If I had to face every fear to get to him, I would without a second thought.

So, I take a deep breath and put one foot in front of the other.

"Excuse me." I get the attention of the receptionist at the front. "Can you tell me what room Collin Mapleson is in?"

She smiles and types on her computer

"Mapleson." She whispers while she scans her screen. After a moment, she looks up at me with a sympathetic smile and my heart feels like it's beating in my ears. "He is still in surgery, miss."

I nod taking a deep breath.

He is still alive.

"But his family is in room 209. Just head to those elevators and go to the second floor."

She gives me a reassuring smile. "Thank you." I fight back tears and turn quickly to the elevators.

Once the elevator doors close, I realize what she said . . . *His family is in room 209.*

Megan.

I am about to meet his sister without him with me.

Trying to calm the butterflies that flutter in my stomach, I watch alone as the elevator number ascends.

I was bound to meet her eventually.

The doors open, bringing a large hallway with a nurse's station into my view. The nurses behind the station do not look up as they are all busy working and running around. So, I look around for room numbers and follow the signs until I am standing in front of a door with 209 written on it.

Raising my fist to knock, I softly knock on the door a few times before gently pressing the handle for the door to open.

A blonde girl jumps out of her seat. I assume this is Megan.

"Is this Collin Mapleson's room?" I ask her.

"Y-yes?" she answers.

"Alyssa?" A voice I haven't heard in forever says my name and it makes all the hair on my arm stand up.

I nod, but his voice brings back memories of my sister. Being in this hospital has taken its toll on me, and I am worried about Collin. My tears flood out of my eyes before I can stop them.

"Is he . . . is he alive?" my voice is hoarse.

Derek's body is rigid, but Megan answers, "Yes, he's in surgery."

I sob.

"And who are you exactly?" Her voice is cold.

"Megan, not now." Derek steps in.

"I don't know who you think you are," Megan starts, "But that is my brother I almost lost today. MY BROTHER!" she yells. "I have a right to know why she is being so dramatic now."

I take a deep breath, knowing I need to introduce myself. Right now, I'd rather it be under any other circumstances.

Holding out my hand to her, I say, "Hey Megan, I have heard a lot about you." I force my tears to stop and try to force a smile. "Collin and I have been dating for a few months now. I was supposed to meet you last night at Hilltop, but I was told you left early when I got there. I hate we are meeting like this."

She stares at me. At first, I think she might tell me to leave, but she stares at my hand right at the tattoo I got a while ago of Collin's initials.

Ugh. I should have worn a sweatshirt.

That tattoo is a reminder. A reminder of what I really was going to do the day I met him and how meeting him changed my whole life.

It reminds me to continue *dodging those curveballs.*

"You can wait with us." She finally tells me but ignores my hand and sits back down.

"Okay then. Great," I say taking a seat beside her.

We all three sit in silence for what seems like forever. Derek won't look at me, and I can't say I blame him. I remind him too much of Haley, as I do to everyone else who used to feel so close to me.

But he reminds me of her, too. The way she would look at him and laugh, or the way both of them were so happy when we found out she was pregnant with my nephew.

Him leaving us the way he did after she died is one of the reasons I think I went down such a dark road. He was all I had left of her, and he abandoned us.

"Megan!!" A brunette-haired girl yells coming in through the door of the hospital room, making all three of us jump out of our skin.

"Maggie!!" Megan is up and hugging her before I can process who she is.

Maggie. She is Collin and Megan's cousin. She came into their life unexpectedly and soon found out she was their long-lost cousin.

I smile. The two hugging almost reminds me of Haley and me. They seem so close, and I hope one day I can have a friend in my life like that.

Maggie turns to us smiling, "Hello. You must be Derek. We haven't officially met, but I'm the one who gave Collin the go ahead to hire you. I'm so glad he did!" She pauses for a moment and smiles wider. "Thank you for taking care of the two people who mean the most to me."

Derek nods but stays quiet.

Her eyes find mine. Butterflies swarm my stomach, anticipating how she is going to react to me seeing as Megan was not too thrilled.

"Are you his girlfriend?" she gestures to Derek, and I have to hide my smirk. I think Derek might faint. "No." Derek and I both say at the same time.

My eyes float to Megan's and anger is written all over her face. Maggie cocks an eyebrow at her, looking confused.

"Maggie," Megan starts, "This is Collin's girlfriend, Alyssa."

I take a deep breath and smile; thankful she did not say anything crude.

"Alyssa, this is our cousin, Maggie. She owns the farm with us." I am shocked, because for the first time since I arrived, Megan has smiled back at me.

It's forced but, hey, it's still there.

Standing nervously, I walk over to Maggie and stick out my hand. "Nice to meet you,

Maggie. Collin has told me a lot about you too." I gulp quickly when her eyes stare at the tattoo on my wrist.

Yep. Should have worn a sweatshirt.

"At least you didn't know about this too, or I would have been even more pissed," Megan snarls.

I take a deep breath; she has been through a lot in the last few hours, and I am sure seeing me here is a shock, too.

Maggie giggles. "Nice to meet you, Alyssa. Please excuse us, we are territorial around here."

They both walk over to the chairs Megan and I were sitting in and sit down and start talking. The only chair left in the room is beside Derek and he looks like he could jump out of his skin at the sight of me right now.

I'll just stand here and wait.

Chapter Fourteen
Alyssa

My stomach started to make this god-awful gurgling sound not long after Maggie showed up. All the cleaning I had done today, and the anxiety of Collin being hurt must have made me burn more calories than I anticipated.

The hospital walls were starting to close in and with Derek here too, it is hard for me to fight the anxiety of the day I lost my sister.

So regretfully, I told everyone I needed to go eat and left the room. When the elevator doors finally closed me inside, taking me to the first floor, I felt like I could breathe a little better again.

While I do not want to miss out on any news that a doctor could come by and give, I also don't want to be in a hospital bed myself.

Following the signs to the cafeteria, I smile as other people pass by me going the opposite direction.

Reaching the cafeteria doors, they open, and the smell of food hits my nose making my stomach grumble more.

Alright, I'll feed you.

I step in line behind some nurses on their break, giving them a soft smile back when they turn to look at me. I see it all over their faces, the sympathy they have toward me. I am sure they can tell I have been crying. It would be hard, working somewhere you see people like me every day. Crying either tears of happiness or sadness.

That's not the kind of job I would want to live every day.

Grabbing a tray, I follow the line and allow the workers behind the buffet bar fill a plate for me with chicken fingers, fries, and a salad. Opening the cooler at the end, I grab a soda bottle. Setting my tray down for the cashier to ring up my order, I hand her some cash. She gives me a sympathetic smile, too, before handing me back my change.

My eyes roam the sitting area for an open table to sit at. I don't make it fully in my seat yet before my phone starts to ring.

"Hello?" I answer quickly not bothering to look at the caller I.D.

"Alyssa!! Are you ok? Is Collin, ok?" Lexi yells on the other end.

I blow out the breath I apparently had been holding and fight back the tears forming at the corner of my eyes. If I could count on anyone to be a friend to me lately, this girl is the one.

"Alyssa? Hello?" she yells again.

My voice breaks. "I- I am here," I whisper.

"Oh, girl. He is going to pull through. He is Collin. He is tough. You just wait. Do you need me to come to the hospital to sit with you?"

My tears flood down my face at that thought alone. To even offer such a thing, to be here for me, I am thankful for the offer even if I don't take it. "No. But thank you for asking." I pause. "Wait, how did you know?"

"Oh, uh . . . Cade told me," Lexi tells me.

I cock an eyebrow. Though she can't see it, I know she can feel it. "So, I am guessing him taking you home last night went well?" I grin.

"Yes," she giggles. "But we aren't talking about me. We are talking about you. What can I do to help?"

I sigh. Right before I tell her nothing, a thought crosses my mind. "Would you and Cade care to run some errands for me? I want Collin to come home with me when he is discharged. Do you both mind cleaning up my apartment for me, grabbing some groceries when we find out when he is coming home, and maybe keep an eye on things for me since Kyle has been showing up?"

"Absolutely!! Your key is still under the plant by the front door?" she asks.

"Yes. And Lexi, thank you. I owe you both. I will Venmo you some money."

She huffs. "Don't you dare. I will not accept it. Keep it and make sure you get food to eat and take care of you. Call me if anything changes."

I close my eyes; a single tear falls down my cheek resting on my lip. That is something my sister would have told me.

***

The elevator door opens to the second floor, and it takes all my strength to step out of it.

I want him to be okay. I want to see his goofy grin again and to hear his voice crack a joke that only his mind can come up with. I want to tell him I love him.

The nurses are all chatting behind the nurse's station as I pass by and while I pass each room, I can hear bits and pieces of conversations inside.

Reaching room 209, I push on the door to open wider and freeze when I see what's before me.

My handsome cowboy is laying in his hospital bed, monitors beeping, and with each beat of his heart, I think mine beats with it.

I quickly wipe a tear before it falls. I want to run to him, throw my arms around him and never leave his side again. But the way Megan is staring at me; I don't move a muscle.

Maggie leans over the bed and whispers something to her. Whatever she says makes Megan huff, but she steps away from the hospital bed allowing me space to see Collin too.

I lean over the bed railing, trailing my fingers around his face and his hairline. I take in every bit of the sight before me because only mere hours ago I thought I would never see it again.

"I am sorry you had to meet my sister this way." His groggy voice makes me smile.

"I don't care. I am just so happy you are okay." I kiss his forehead.

"I love you, pretty girl."

I gasp, my heart hammers in my chest. "I never thought I'd have the chance to tell you that." He whispers, "Just in case, I need you to know that."

Tears fall down my cheek and fall onto his hospital gown. "You will have the rest of your life to tell me, but I love you, too."

He smiles and falls back into a deep slumber.

Chapter Fifteen
Collin

I don't care how cute and cuddly those damn wild animals look.

They are not cute when they pounce on your femoral artery and almost kill you. If it had not been for Derek being out there with me, I am sure I would have died.

My grandfather once told me, *"Son, don't put all your trust in an animal. Even the horses we ride have a mind of their own."*

"Go home." I hear Megan tell Maggie. "You have an infant and a husband at home who need you. Logan will need to take care of the farm while I help Collin recover. If I need you, I will call. Please go home and take care of yourself. You are not even six weeks postpartum yet."

The two women who have been nothing but a blessing in my life hug and Maggie walks over to me. "Don't you dare go trying to get yourself killed again. I don't think my hormones can take anymore."

She leans into me, kissing my forehead. "I love you, goober."

"Ewe. My goober should not be in your mind." I grin and she swats at me.

"Thankful to have your goofy self back." She quickly laughs and rolls her eyes.

"I love you too." I smile.

Megan walks her out and I look around the empty hospital room, knowing when my sister comes back that we need to have a talk.

"Where are Alyssa and Derek?" I ask Megan when she walks back in while shutting the door behind her.

"Derek is at the farm helping Logan and Alyssa is down at the cafeteria getting some food," she huffs, fixing my blanket on the bed at my feet. "The girl won't leave. I have tried to get her to go home but she won't. Will you tell her?"

"No, I won't. I want her here with me."

Megan looks at me with a look only she can give. She is fighting a war in her mind right now and I am just thankful I am hurt in the hospital bed or that may be where I would end up from talking back to her.

"Collin, she can come see you at the farm when you get home. It's my job to take care of you. Honestly, you hid her from me. You must not think too much of her anyway."

I try to sit up a little. My leg is in a sling above the bed holding it in a cast, so I only move a little. "This is why I hid her from you, Megan. You don't think anyone else can care for me the way you do."

"They can't," she growls.

I huff, "I love you, Meg. You basically raised me, but I am not some little boy anymore. I am a man with dreams and a life I want for myself. And that includes Alyssa."

"It has always been you and me," she mumbles. "And when we lost our parents, I couldn't imagine not having you by my side."

"You are going to always have me at your side. But I need to live my own life and make my own place. My home will always be the farm. But Alyssa is slowly showing me I can have a home with her, too." I pause making sure she understands this next part. "When you disrespect her, you are disrespecting me. Please don't make me choose. Because I will choose her."

Megan looks like she is about to yell at me, but the door opens and a woman wearing bright pink scrubs walks in with a smile that quickly fades when she sees Megan's face. "Therapy," she says. "Is this a bad time?"

"No," I grin. "Perfect timing. What do you have for me today?"

She laughs. "A lot of pain."

I huff. "Great because pain is my middle name."

The woman walks around to the side of my bed and laughs. "I have a feeling you are going to be one of my favorites."

***

Alyssa

I can hear someone moving around in the room while I stir awake. The cot I have been sleeping on this past week while at the hospital has not been the best, but it kept me close to my guy and that's all I care about. If I had to sleep on the cold tile floor, I would have.

The sun has just started to rise. I rub my eyes a few times to get them to open and see Megan moving around me. She must have heard me move because she looks at me and whispers, "I am just going to get some coffee."

When the door shuts behind her, I look up at my guy resting. He has had a wonderful week of therapy, and the doctors said last night that he would be able to go home today.

Home.

While I know Megan will want him to go back to the farm with her, I want him to come home with me. Let me show Megan that I can take care of him the way she can. I want her to know I am here for the long haul.

Standing up from my cot, I let out a big stretch and walk over to Collin laying in the bed, kissing his forehead. His eyes flutter but he stays sound asleep.

Making my way out into the hallway, I spot Megan by the coffee machine that the nurses have left out for us every morning this week and take a deep breath before I approach. What I am about to ask her is not something I take lightly.

"Um, Megan?" My voice is still raspy from sleep. I clear my throat a few times.

She jumps. "Alyssa," she grabs her chest, "That is a good way to get hit."

While I hope she is kidding, a part of me doesn't think she is. Her back turns on me continuing to pour sugar and creamer in her cup.

"I'm sorry," I tell her. "I just wanted to talk to you for a minute."

She sighs. I have a feeling she knows what I am about to ask. "What is it?"

"Well, Collin is going to need some extensive therapy." I pause, giving her a minute to process. "And he will need to be looked after all day until he can put weight on his foot again. The doctors are saying it could take up to six weeks or more."

She nods but stays silent.

I take in a deep breath of air and release it. "Well, I live not far from here. And I want to offer to let Collin move in with me. I know you have big responsibilities at the farm and not enough help as it is." I pull nervously on a few strands of hair. "I want to take care of him, and he will be in good hands."

She stares back at me, and I cannot read her look. A part of her looks angered but the other part looks almost...thankful.

Finally, she lets a soft, but strained, grin run across her face. "Give me a few minutes to think about it."

I nod, feeling defeated. But I refuse to show it, so I grab a cup of coffee, even though I don't drink the stuff hot, and make my way back into Collin's room.

Collin still lays asleep peacefully when I enter his room. For a few moments, I watch him sleep. His chest rising and falling, the monitors beeping with his heart, and I cannot help but feel thankful.

After losing Haley and then going through the abuse I did from Kyle, I never thought I would be happy again.

Until this goofy cowboy walked into my life. If I had lost him, I don't know if I would have survived it.

He has become my best friend.

I set down my cup of coffee on his bedside table and sit in the chair beside him. A brochure about therapy that one of the nurses brought in lays on the table, too, and I grab it. Opening it up, I read over the parts about therapy and what to expect with the type of recovery he will have.

I look up when the door opens and Megan walks in. She looks at me and then back to her brother. I don't miss the quick second of wiping her tear away. I know how much her brother means to her; Haley meant that much to me.

I wipe a tear from my own eye watching him lay there, too.

"You really care about him, don't you?" she asks me.

I nod.

"Promise me I won't regret what I am about to say," she starts. My eyes turn hopeful. "I promise you, if something happens to him, I will hunt you down and make you wish you were never born."

Did she just threaten me? Yes. Do I care? Not in the slightest. Because my cowboy gets to come *home* with me.

I jump up and wrap my arms around Megan who stiffens within my touch.

"Thank you! I promise I will update you all the time, and you are welcome to come visit anytime." I step in to hug her again and she puts her hand up to stop me.

Fair enough.

"Yes, keep me updated. And I will give you Maggie's number too. If you cannot get me, call her."

I nod, pulling out my phone so we can exchange numbers.

I smile at my phone when her text comes through. "I know you are not too sure about me right now, but one day I hope to be friends with you and Maggie."

I give her a smile and go back to sit beside Collin.

"What did I miss?" My sleepy cowboy asks, half asleep.

"You're going to be moving into my place," I tell him excitedly.

He smiles big and pulls me into a kiss, whispering. "I thought I already had."

Pulling out of our kiss he looks at his sister and speaks. "I am shocked the warden let that fly."

"Don't worry, I have already threatened her." Megan winks and Collin laughs.

But I don't move a muscle.

Chapter Sixteen
Collin

A week has passed, and I get to go home.

Funny, *home* use to be the farm. And if I was in the same situation right now a year ago—no, five months ago, I would have thought home would be the farm.

But it's not. Home is wherever Alyssa is.

I am grateful Megan could not run Alyssa off this week. My girl stood her ground with my sister, and it makes me even more thankful she is mine. Secretly, I think Megan has grown to have some respect for her this week, too, watching Alyssa help me, care for me, and never leaving my side. Actually, I know she has, because if she hadn't, I would be heading to Magnolia Farms right now, not Alyssa's apartment.

Megan stands beside me under the awning of the hospital while Alyssa goes to grab her car from the parking lot. I shift around in the wheelchair they made me get in. I wanted to walk out on my crutches, but the nurses refused to let me leave unless I was wheeled out.

My ass has never moved so fast to sit in a wheelchair in my life.

I just want to go *home.*

Plus, I would be lying if I said I hadn't been thinking about having my girl to myself. Just because I am on crutches doesn't mean we can't keep *playing*.

She has been doing all the work lately anyway. It would be a shame if I let her get rusty on my accord.

Megan's swaying side to side beside me; her sign of being anxious. I reach out to grab her hand. I know how much not being in control of me is going to cause her pain. I have been her little shadow since the day I was born. She may be a pain in my ass, but she is the reason I am who I am today.

"I love her," I say with a grin.

Her eyes glisten with a tear.

"Thank you for letting me fly away from the nest," I say.

She tightens the grip of her hand in mine and says, "You know you always have a place to call home."

I nod with a big smile.

Alyssa pulls under the awning in front of us before we notice Derek's truck pulling in behind her.

"Maggie sent me to pick you up," Derek says to Megan jumping out of his truck and shutting the door.

He walks over to me, giving me his hand to shake. "I am glad you are okay, brother."

"I have you to thank for that," I tell him grabbing his hand and pulling him in for a hug.

Derek looks shocked when we pull out of our hug but finally laughs. "I knew she would kill me if I let anything happen to you."

I smirk at my sister who is snarling at him. She may really end up killing him while I am gone.

RIP, brother, if I never see you again.

The three of them all help me out of the wheelchair and into Alyssa's car. Megan slides the crutches in beside my legs and gives me one last hug before shutting the door.

I take a deep breath, watching the one woman who's been a constant in my life since I was born fall back in the rear-view mirror behind us. Alyssa slips into the driver's seat, getting my attention, and I look at the new woman in my life—the one I want to spend the rest of my life with.

This isn't me saying goodbye to my family—it's me wanting to have my own life and family with the woman I love.

This is what it means to grow up.

"Ready?" Alyssa smiles at me.

I nod, leaning over and grabbing her chin, pulling her into me and kissing her softly.

"Let's go home," I tell her.

***

"Welcome Home!" Cade and Lexie yell when Alyssa and I walk through the front door. Well, Alyssa walked through the door. I was hopping on one foot and crutches, but who's keeping score?

A welcome home banner hangs over the wall of the living room, a casserole is on the stove, and I know for a fact it's from Nana's from the smell alone.

"Guys!!" Alyssa squeals and runs to Lexie, giving her a big hug. "You didn't have to do all of this."

"We were here cleaning anyways. Plus, it's a big deal to have you home brother," Cade says pulling me into a hug.

I smile, clapping him on the back. A little wobbly with the crutches, but thankfully he noticed and kept me balanced.

"Thank you, man," I tell him. Cade has been one of my closest friends since high school.

"Any updates on Kyle since I have been preoccupied?" I whisper in his ear, so the girls won't hear.

He nods. "I will tell you later or call you. Don't want to freak the girls out."

We follow the girls in the kitchen, and I find a seat in one of the kitchen table chairs. The cast on my leg is starting to get heavy the longer I am up.

"You guys want to sit and eat with us?" Alyssa asks Lexie and Cade while she pulls down plates from the cabinet.

They look at each other and back at her. "No," they say in unison.

I laugh. "Oh, I see. I missed something."

Lexie's face blushes and Cade clears his throat. "We are going to go and get out of your hair. I am sure you both want to be alone."

Lexie winks at Alyssa and Cade bends to hug me one more time. "I will call you later, brother. Get some rest."

I don't miss the butt slap Lexie gets from Cade before they close the door behind them.

"Are they?" I ask Alyssa raising my eyebrow.

"A lady never tells." She winks sitting my plate of casserole in front of me.

I grab her forearm and pull her onto my lap. "Is that right?"

"Collin! Your leg! Oh my gosh, let me up. I am going to hurt you!"

I giggle. "You are not going to hurt me. Sit. I have missed having you close to me."

Her eyes widen. "Collin. You cannot seriously have a boner right now."

I smirk. "Get ready babe. Handicap doggy style coming your way."

She laughs hoarsely and smacks me across the chest. "You are full of it."

"Full of love for you." I smile, crashing my lips onto hers.

Chapter Seventeen
Alyssa

I position my body weight on his good leg while poking the fork into the casserole on the plate I made and feed it to him.

Collin smiles with each bite. "How about I feed you the other half?"

He takes the fork from me, scrapes some casserole onto it, and moves it to my mouth. I open wide, allowing the deliciousness to tingle all my sinuses.

The hospital cafeteria food was alright, but nothing beats food from Nana's.

It is even better than Patsy's, where I work.

He brings another bite close to my mouth but moves it quickly, turning the fork upside down making the food fall onto my shoulder near my neck.

I am thankful it's not hot or my skin would be burned.

"Collin!" I squeal but he ignores me, dipping his head down to lick up the food on my skin. "Collin," I moan. "You . . ." my breath is labored, "We cannot do anything until you recover."

He pulls back my shirt, revealing more skin, and nips at my collarbone. "Who said that?"

I fight the urge to fully turn around and straddle him. "Well, I guess technically no one. But the doctor did say to rest."

"I rest better post orgasm."

He is not playing fair.

"But your leg." I whisper my eyes closing every time his mouth touches my skin.

He grabs my waist and in one quick move, he has me facing him with my legs on either side of his body. "Looks to me like you can do all the work from here, Madame."

I throw my head back in a hoarse laugh. *How do I say no to this man?*

He lifts my shirt up, exposing my stomach, bra, and eventually it falls to the floor beside us.

"Oops." He grins at me. That boyish grin I have come to love and adore.

"I need to take a shower," I tell him. Although I did use the shower in his hospital room this week to wash off, I still feel dirty. I feel the hospital is all over me.

"I listened to you shower last night," he winks.

"Ugh. Nothing gets by you." I roll my eyes.

"Not when it comes to you."

I slide off him, my eyes narrowing on the bulge in his pants. The sight of it makes me even more wet.

I have missed him.

Grabbing the button of my pants, I glide the zipper down and shimmy out of my jeans. His feral eyes don't leave me for a second. His pupils growing darker with each piece of fabric I remove.

Standing in front of him in my bra and panties I smirk. "Looks to me like we have a problem."

He frowns. "What?"

"You are sitting down with your sweatpants on," I smirk.

He grabs his crutches, impressively fast, and hops up from his chair. "Slide these fuckers off."

His urgent request makes me giggle. "Come into the living room."

He doesn't hesitate at all. The crutches click across the floor as he makes his way to the couch and stands in front of it. "I am not sitting until they are off."

I bite my lip, fighting to hold back my laugh. I could be so mean right now. I could tease him and never do what he asks. But as much fun as that would be, I want to feel him inside me. A week ago, I thought that might never happen again.

Grabbing the waist of his sweats, I shimmy them, along with his boxers, down his thighs. His cast makes it hard to get them over the top of it and he grunts. "Leave them. All you need is my dick out anyways." Collin lowers himself to the couch and sits down, throwing his crutches across the room. His hungry eyes focus on me.

My heart hammers in my chest. Climbing onto the couch, I straddle him. My panties the only thing keeping us separate.

"Now, Mr. Mapleson. I have missed you." I bend down to kiss him.

First, it's soft, until he parts my lips with his tongue, stealing my breath with it.

While he is lost in our kiss, I reach down, moving the fabric that is keeping us separate to the side and fully impale myself on his length.

We moan into each other's mouths as the sensation takes us over.

"I love you," Collin purrs.

I grin into his lips. "I love you."

Using my thighs, I lift myself up and back down making sure to take all of him in my warmth. My rhythm starts slow but when his hands go to my hips, I quickly increase my speed.

"You are soaked baby," he moans. "You feel so good."

His words make my eyes roll back into my head. He feels good, too.

"Is your leg, okay?" I ask him, in between my labored breaths.

"If you don't stop worrying about that fucking leg," he says with a snarl, and I can't explain what happens after that. My heart rate starts flying through me, I jump off him and run to the bathroom.

Slamming the door behind me, I lock it and grab the sink to steady myself. My eyes look terrified in the mirror, and tunnel vision takes over me.

He is not Kyle. He is not Kyle. He is not Kyle.
I remind myself.

I hear something crash in the living room and it brings me back to where I am.

I am home. I am safe. I am with Collin.

He is not Kyle. He is not Kyle.

Then I remember his leg, his crutches, and the sound that I just heard in the living room sounded like something or someone fell.

Opening the door, I rush out and find Collin on the floor, trying to get back up.

"I forgot my fucking leg was in a cast and went after you." His tone is clipped. "I am so sorry Alyssa. I wasn't thinking. I would never hurt you."

A tear creases the corner of my eye.

I know he won't.

He is not Kyle.

He is not Kyle.

He is not Kyle.

Chapter Eighteen
Collin

I know I scared her. And I hate myself for saying those words. I have never cussed at her but as much as a crappy excuse as it is, I got lost in the moment and got carried away.

Again—a crappy excuse.

I should have been better. I should have known better.

But I missed my girl. I missed being inside her. I missed her body and the way it felt close to mine. And I missed being alone with her.

Seeing her cry last night was worse than the bob cat attacking me.

We went to bed shortly after and she didn't say much. She also left for work this morning without much to say either besides, "I love you, bye."

So, I sit here, flipping through channels on the tv, wondering how to make it up to her.

My phone buzzes beside me on the couch startling me.

"Hey man," I tell Cade on the other end.

"Hey brother. How was your first night home?"

I lie. "It was good. Slept well."

Actually, I slept like shit, but he doesn't have to know that.

"Well, I can't talk long. But I wanted to give you a heads up. Alyssa called Lexie and asked for us to clean up the place before you got to come home. So, the next day, we came over and cleaned up."

"Yeah, she was so thankful you both could do that." I tell him.

"Anytime man," he starts, "But the thing is, I got there before Lexie. She got called into work for morning shift. When I arrived, Alyssa's door was wide open."

I sit up, not liking where this is going.

"I was in my police cruiser, so I grabbed my pistol and walked in. Lexie had told me where the spare key was in case, I arrived before her. It was still there under the pot, but the door hadn't been busted or anything. So, I think someone used it and then put it back. Making it look like she had purposely left it open." He paused. "I walked through, and no one was inside but things were trashed. It seemed like whoever it was needed to find something or was pissed off she was not home."

"Did you pull video from the cameras around the building?" I ask.

"That's another thing. I went to the main office, and they told me the cameras had been cut that morning. They were working to get them back up and running."

"For fuck's sake." I rub my hand over my face.

"I didn't tell Lexie because I didn't want her to worry, but I would put money on it being that Kyle guy. Has he shown his face anymore?"

"Not that I know of, but I kind of have been preoccupied this last week," I answer.

"Right. Well, I have deputies hanging around her place until we know for sure. I worked up a report, too, just in case. I was going to tell you so you could tell Alyssa. It would be best coming from you."

I sigh. Right now, that's the last thing she needs to know about. But I also agree she needs to know. "Yeah, thanks man."

"I will call you if I hear of anything else," he says. "And Collin?"

"Yeah?"

"Get the girl some shooting lessons. You can use the range at the department. Just let me know beforehand before you come."

"Thanks man, I will. Be safe out there. And I don't mean just with work. With Lexie, too," I joke.

He chuckles. "10/4 buddy."

***

I am asleep on the couch when the front door shutting startles me awake.

Jumping up, I panic, first thinking about what Cade said, eventually realizing it's Alyssa coming in from her shift.

I give her a gentle grin. "How was your day?"

She only worked half a shift today and will be off tomorrow. My body is used to working all day from sunup to sundown. The walls of this apartment are starting to close in on me already.

"It was good. How are you feeling?" she asks, setting her purse down on the coffee table and walking over to the couch to sit by me.

"Better now that you are home." I grab her hand and hold it in mine. "I am so sorry about last night."

She gives me a soft smile. "I know you are. And I am sorry, too. I don't know what happened. My brain can't decipher the difference between safe and harm. It's like the words made me transport back in time and my mind was saying 'this is too much like before. Abort mission.'"

"And I want you to know, how you felt is okay. You are safe and you are loved, and I will never do that again." My thumb runs across her hand.

"Thank you for being so supportive." She leans into me, kissing my cheek.

I debate on waiting to tell her about Kyle, but she deserves to know the truth. I would want her to be honest with me so I should give her the same honesty in return.

"I need to tell you something that I don't want to scare you. It is for your safety." My eyes hold hers and I hope this doesn't cause her to panic again.

Sighing, I take a deep breath. "Cade said when he came over to clean the house the day after you came to the hospital, your front door was wide open, and things were a mess inside."

At first, she looks confused, but then her eyes widen.

"He said no one was inside and the spare key was still under the pot. The door was still intact so either someone picked the lock or knew where the key was."

Her hands start to feel sweaty. "Hey. Look at me. We don't know if it was him."

"But who else would it be, Collin? You heard him the night at Hilltop. He is not going to stop." She is about to bolt. I can feel it.

"Come here." I pull her into me, wrapping my arms around her. "You are safe. And you will always be safe as long as I am here. But I do think we need to get you some shooting lessons."

"I don't know if I could shoot anyone," she whispers.

"You could if it meant surviving." I rub her shoulder. "You are off tomorrow. We can go and let you practice."

She nods her head wiping a tear. "I wish I never met him. I wish I could go back in time and walk the other direction. Sometimes I replay that moment in my head and purposely walk away hoping it will become my new reality."

I kiss the top of her head. "But meeting him is what led you to me. You went through the things you did to get here and be present now. And you will get past this little speed bump."

"I will dodge this curveball," she mumbles.

"You most definitely will dodge it," I say laying my head on top of hers with a smile.

Chapter Nineteen
Alyssa

The shooting range at the Maple Police Department is in a large open field behind the station.

An awning with four picnic tables and cooler full of drinks stands before the range starts. Target cutouts of humans are at the end of the range about fifteen to twenty yards away.

Collin leans his crutches against the picnic table and climbs up on the top, taking a seat. "Alright, pretty girl. Let's see what you got." He unclips my pistol from his side and checks the clip.

"This is your safety." He tells me pointing at a small button behind the trigger. It shows a white dot at the moment, but the second he hits the button, the dot turns red. "The red dot means the safety is off and you can shoot. You do not turn the safety off until you are ready to pull the trigger."

I nod getting closer to him so I can pay attention.

He flips the safety back on and holds it up to me. "This is your trigger." He points to the obvious part of the whole gun. The part that scares me.

"You do not put your finger on this until you are ready to fire." He holds the pistol up like he is going to shoot but keeps his finger off the trigger. Instead, he lays it beside the length of the gun where the chamber is.

"This is how you should hold the gun until you are ready to pull the trigger." He hands the gun to me. "Go stand over there and let me see how you hold it. Don't shoot yet."

I grab it from him with shaky hands. The day I bought this gun I was scared. I never intended on using it, but it was more of a reassurance for myself that I had it in case I needed to.

Standing near the edge of the pavilion, I square my legs, holding my arms straight out and gun in my hands, remembering to keep the safety on and my finger off the trigger like Collin said.

"Man, you look beautiful like that." Collin smiles at me.

"I am terrified," I tell him.

He chuckles. "Don't be. You are in control. It is something new and anxious nerves are normal. But knowledge is power. You should always have the knowledge to protect yourself.

I hope you never have to use it, but it makes me feel better knowing you can if you ever need to."

He grabs his crutches and slides off the picnic table, making his way over to me. "Now, assess your target."

I look at the target ahead of me and take a deep breath.

I can do this.

"When you feel good about it, click the safety off like I showed you. Don't do anything yet. One step at a time," he assures me.

I blow out a breath, thankful for his patience. Clicking the safety off, I relax my shoulders and find my target again.

"Good. Now take a deep breath and when you release, I want you to pull the trigger. Make sure you are aiming at the target."

Taking a deep breath, I fill my lungs with air and on the release of it, my fingers grab the trigger, an explosion rattling my ears.

"Oh shit!" I yell. The gun flies from my hands and across the ground beside us.

"Well, that's one way to get shot," Collin laughs.

"Sorry." My cheeks flush with embarrassment. "I didn't realize it would be that forceful."

"I should have warned you," he chuckles, hopping over on his crutches to pick it up. He inspects it and laughs. "Next time, hold on to it."

"Yes, sir," I grin.

Handing it to me he orders, "Try again. I doubt you even hit the target with the grip you had on it."

Something about this time, I feel more confident and in control. This time, I know what to expect. I take aim again, looking at my target.

This go around; the target isn't just a paper cut out. It's Kyle. He is smirking at me the way he would when he knew he had me in his grips. His evil eyes staring into me the way they would when he would rape me. The laugh he would give when he knew he won.

I take a deep breath and on release I pull the trigger.

"Holy shit," Collin exclaims. "Perfect shot!"

I pull the gun down and clip the safety back on. Running to the target, I can't believe my eyes.

Bullseye.

The bullet hit right at the heart.

I fall to my knees, holding my face in my hands.

I can survive this. I can beat him. I can protect myself.

Collin's crutches come up behind me. "You okay, pretty girl?"

I jump to my feet and run to my cowboy, slinging my arms around him. "Thank you for doing this for me. All I needed was for someone to believe in me and make me feel safe."

He rubs my back and leans his head into my neck. "You are worth believing in, pretty girl."

Chapter Twenty
Collin

A week has passed since the shooting range. The confidence I have seen in Alyssa has been remarkable and something I will cherish forever.

Something snapped inside her. She doesn't seem as scared out in public or at home anymore.

She kicks her feet in the chair beside me as we sit in the doctor's office for my checkup.

"Collin Mapleson." The nurse calls my name and Alyssa hands me my crutches, helping me stand before we follow the nurse down the hall into the exam room.

"How have you been, Mr. Mapleson?" the petite older woman asks me. Her hair is short and grey. Her scrubs are purple, and she looks like burnout would be her middle name.

I smile. "Great. Just ready to get this cast off."

She laughs. "Today might be your lucky day." She types something into the computer and stands, excusing herself before shutting the door behind her.

"That is exciting!" Alyssa squeals.

"Therapy is going well. I bet they get to take it off and put something more moveable on."

She is right. Therapy is going well. But there is only so much I can do with this big cast on. I was told if I kept improving, I may get it off early.

Let's hope today is that day.

"Mr. Mapleson." An older man with grey hair and bushy eyebrows walks in wearing a white lab coat, suit pants, and tie. "Glad to see you doing so well. You sure gave us a scare a few weeks ago."

"Good to see you again, Doctor Kilmer." Alyssa puts out her hand for him to shake.

I don't remember this man. But I also do not remember many people from the hospital. The staff were all wonderful Megan and Alyssa told me, but their faces and names are all still fuzzy in my mind.

He shakes Alyssa's hand with a smile and turns to me. "You were high on pain meds the last time I saw you, so you most likely don't remember me. I am the doctor who performed your surgery."

I shake his hand and nod. "Nice to meet you."

He pulls up my chart and clicks on the x-rays I took yesterday at therapy. "Looks wonderful." He clicks around the picture zooming in and out. "I'd say let's get that cast off today."

Alyssa squeals. "Really?"

He grins. "Unless Mr. Mapleson would like to keep it on another week."

"Fuck, no," I blurt out and Alyssa slaps my thigh. "I mean, no sir," I smirk.

He throws his head back in a laugh. "Alrighty then. Let me go get the cast tech to bring in the supplies for removal. I want to see you back in two weeks. Until then, you can use a prophylactic brace. It'll allow you more movement so you can start doing more exercises at therapy."

"Thank you." I hold my hand out for him to shake.

"Any more questions?" he asks.

"One." I start and grin, knowing this is going to embarrass Alyssa. "Is doggy style okay for us now?"

"Collin Mapleson!!" Alyssa screeches.

"As long as you support that leg, you can slowly go back to regular activities. No heavy lifting until I see you again." He laughs, closing the door behind him.

"I am going to beat you!" she yells at me when we are alone again.

"Sounds like fun, madame." I wink.

***

Lexie brings us our order, setting it down in front of us. After my appointment, we both decided we were low on fuel and needed something to eat. While I would prefer Nana's, Patsy's was closer.

"What else can I get you?" she asks.

"Nothing. Thank you, Lex." Alyssa smiles at her.

My leg feels funny with the cast off. At first when the cast tech walked in, my eyes widened when I saw the saw in her hand. I guess I never really thought about how they were going to get it off. Fortunately, it was a piece of cake. Just loud and shook my leg to death.

My incision is healing nicely, too, and from the X-rays, all the work done on the inside looks like it is healing nicely.

This new brace allows me to bend my knee freely and it's such a good feeling to be able to do that again. I still cannot put much weight on my leg, but the doctor said that would come with time and therapy.

"I am starving!" Alyssa says scarfing down her chicken fingers and fries. I laugh watching her eat like she hasn't had a meal in years.

"You are cute when you stuff your face like that," I wink at her.

"Oh, don't you dare joke now. You are still in trouble for that question you asked the doctor."

"It was an important question," I smirked.

"It was not!" she squeals.

I take a few bites of my chicken fingers and fries too, washing them down with the soda I ordered. "You are cute when you get flustered."

Her cheeks turn pink. "I am not flustered!"

"Are too!" I stick my tongue out at her.

My phone rings in my pocket and Megan's name reads across the screen.

"Hey Meg!" I answer.

"Collin!" she sounds worn out. "I just wanted to let you know. Maggie is having to have emergency surgery. Her bladder prolapsed and Derek found her in the barn. I have Rhett and everything is okay here. I will keep you updated."

"Whoa, that was a lot of information all at once." Alyssa looks at me concerned. "Do I need to come that way?"

Megan laughs. "And have you to worry about, too? Nah, I got it under control. I got Alyssa's text a little bit ago. Glad the big cast got to come off."

"Me, too. He said we can do doggy now." I wink at Alyssa, and she looks mortified.

"Ewww. I did not need to know that!" she snarls.

I smirk. "Well, just keeping you updated!"

"About your sex life? Yeah, I don't care to know about that." I hear Rhett crying in the background. "I got to go. Tell Alyssa I said hi! Love you!"

"Love you, too!" I tell her before hanging up the phone.

"You did not just tell your sister that!" Alyssa looks like she wants to hit me.

"That I love her? Absolutely." I grin.

Her napkin hits my face as I dive back into my food.

Chapter Twenty-One
Alyssa

The road that leads to my apartment is empty when I turn on it, following the winding path back into the woods where the buildings all sit.

Parking in my designated parking spot, I jump out and jog around the car to Collin's side, grab his crutches from the back seat, and hand them to him.

My feet halt when we reach the front door, and I see a note taped to the front on a piece of torn notebook paper.

Written in red are the words: **YOU WILL NEVER ESCAPE ME.**

Collin yanks it off the door and pulls his phone out, calling someone.

"Cade. Get over to Alyssa's. NOW!" He hangs up not giving Cade a chance to reply.

"Get inside," he orders me, looking around at our surroundings.

Stepping inside, I am thankful I moved the hide a key. Well, technically I didn't really "move it", I gave it to Lexie in case I ever needed her to get inside.

Collin hops in behind me, shutting the door and locking it. "Fucker is going to get what is coming to him." He looks at me. "Are you okay?"

I nod taking a deep breath.

"You need to start keeping your gun on you again," he tells me.

I carried it with me for a while but eventually started leaving it in my car instead of on me.

In no time, a knock is coming from my front door. Collin hops over and looks through the peep hole before unlocking it and allowing Cade to step inside.

"What is wrong?" Cade asks. He must be on duty because he is in uniform.

Collin shoves the note left on the door at him. Cade looks over it and then back at me. "Are you okay?"

I nod my head, yes, and he turns back to Collin. "I'll go see if I can get a look at the security cameras. Stay here."

No more than fifteen minutes later, Cade is walking back inside the apartment with a sour look on his face. "It's him."

Collin lets out a breath, his nostrils flaring. "Can you arrest him for it?"

Cade looks defeated. "Unfortunately, no. He didn't break in. There's not a 'no trespassing' sign. He did nothing illegal."

"He threatened me." I point at the paper.

"But he didn't act on the threat. Unless he acts on the threat, I cannot legally do anything."

He looks as disappointed as we do. "Believe me, I want to get this son of a bitch as much as you both do. But we must be smart about it. If we do something that sets him off, he could get dangerous. I don't agree with it any more than you do but there are policies I cannot override."

Collin runs his hands through his hair. "What if it was Lexie?"

Cades eyes turn sad. "If it was Lexie, I would teach her how to defend herself. I would have police watching her home. I would make her keep a gun on her. And I would hope and pray to God he messes up before she had to use it."

The look he gives Collin tells me all I need to know. He is telling Collin that is what I should do.

"I'll have a cruiser sitting out here tonight. I got some 'no trespassing' signs in my car. I'll bring one and put it out front. That way, if he does come back, we will have something to get him for."

Cade turns to me. "In the meantime, I don't advise you going anywhere alone or without protection. This guy is smart. Has he hurt you before?"

I nod. "Yes."

"When?" his sad eyes hold mine.

"Not anytime in the last few months."

He squeezes my shoulder. "We will get him."

"Thank you." I mouth, fighting back tears.

"Thanks man." Collin holds his hand out for Cade to shake.

Cade grabs his hand and shakes it. "Call me anytime, day or night."

***

"Can you sleep?" I ask the big bear of a man lying beside me.

He snorts. "Nope. How about you?"

"Every time I hear a sound outside; I think it's him coming in." I release a breath.

"Me too," Collin admits.

His hand runs up my waist and pull me into him. I feel his erection against my butt and before I realize it, I am nuzzling it farther into him.

He mumbles in my ear, "Does Madame want to play?"

I smile. Do I? The last time I ran out of the room. I am afraid of it happening again. He hasn't pushed me about it since. Yes, he jokes, but he has left the physical part all to me. Something I truly never knew guys were capable of.

The day at the shooting range changed something inside me, though. I feel less…weak.

I am coming to terms with things happening in life to make me who I am today. And for the better part of the last year, I allowed my emotions to stop me from looking at how to overcome it.

I cowered down and let it make me a victim when I should have allowed it to show me how to be a survivor.

Collin met a woman a girl with a broken heart—that he did not break. He could have said, 'She is too damaged. She is not worth the time. She is going to be hard to get through to.'

Instead, he met me where I was, walked with me every step forward, and step back, I took. He allowed me to feel the things I felt but never allowed me to stay there.

He has protected me from the day I met him.

I roll over, facing him, allowing my lips to reach up and touch his briefly. He pulls back from me raising an eyebrow curiously but stays silent.

"How about tonight, I let you take control?" I grin at him.

He bites his lips to stop his smile. "Are you sure?"

"I am ready," I tell him.

"If you want me to stop, just say the word," he assures me.

Instead of answering him with words, I scoot further into him, my lips crashing back on his. He parts our lips with his tongue, massaging mine.

His hands stop at my hips pulling me closer to him. The t-shirt I slept in tonight gives him easy access when he lowers his hand under it pulling at my panties. His fingers dip underneath my underwear and he grins into our kiss. "Someone is all wet."

I moan into his touch. He runs his fingers into my wetness before slipping two fingers in at once inside me. My head falls back at the feeling of him.

"Such a tight, beautiful pussy," he whispers into my ear.

"How is your leg?" I ask before I realize what happened last time.

He smiles. "Able to handle what I am about to do to you."

He removes his fingers rolling me onto my stomach grabbing my hips and putting me in a doggy style position.

I cannot help but laugh. I guess my guy is about to get his wish.

He grabs a pillow to prop his leg on. With his good knee bent, the other leg is laid out straight to the side of the pillow. "See? It's protected."

I laugh. "Well, I am glad."

Somehow between grabbing the pillows and propping his leg up, he also is butt naked. Pulling my panties down, Collin pushes my t-shirt up my back and lines his tip to my entrance letting it glide through my wetness.

"Collin. Please," I beg.

"Don't have to beg me twice," he laughs. In one swift thrust, he slams into me, making me see stars for a few minutes while I adjust to his size.

"Welcome home to me," he moans.

Grabbing my hips, he steadies himself behind me while his pumps grow more hectic. Reaching under my waist, he lifts me up flush with his chest and whispers into my ear, "Mine. You are mine."

"I am yours," I promise.

He gathers my t-shirt and pulls it off over my head throwing it on the floor. I also didn't go to bed in a bra. What sane woman does?

His fingers reach up, grabbing my breasts and squeezing my right nipple. The pain is all I need for my orgasm to rip through me.

'Milk me, pretty girl.' Collin moans behind me, his thrusts starting to become faster.

The warmth of his seeds flows into me as his own explosion takes over.

"Doggy style is my new favorite thing." He kisses my neck.

Chapter Twenty-Two
Collin

I remember being a little boy, watching my grandparents kiss and hug, hoping one day I would have that type of love too.

It was a sad day when the two people who raised us kids passed away, but the fact they left this earth together is a true testament to the love they shared.

I also grew up listening to stories of the love my parents shared. Megan would tell me how our father worshipped the ground our mother walked on, and I will always believe their love is the reason Megan and I have always found strength in one another.

Losing our parents at a young age was tragic, it is something I wouldn't wish on my worst enemy, but it made me value the meaning of family.

The meaning of telling those I love that I love them when I have the chance to and not waiting until I can't.

That bob cat reminded me of that too. I remember how scared I was right before I stopped breathing; I thought I would never see my girl standing before me again. I promised myself if I got a second chance, I would spend it cherishing her.

Other than my boneheaded mistake the other night, I like to believe I have kept good on my promise.

Alyssa applies her eye shadow and grins at me. "You just going to watch me the whole time?"

"Pretty much," I wink at her.

She rolls her eyes and goes back to fixing her makeup.

As much as I hate it, she has to go into work today. Kyle is still hanging around and it makes me feel uneasy not knowing exactly where he is.

"Keep your pistol in your purse," I tell her.

She nods. "Already there. It's just half a shift, Collin. I will be fine."

I know she will be, but if I could strap myself to her, I would.

"What do you got planned today?"

"Wait for you to return." She rolls her eyes at that remark, and I laugh, grabbing my crutches and turning back down the hall toward the living room. "Honestly, I might call Cade and see if he's heard of anything since the note."

"Don't stress too much," she says walking out of the bathroom dressed and ready for her shift. "He is doing the best he can."

"I will relax when that fucker is gone," I state honestly. And it's the truth. He has caused nothing but bad things for my girl.

She leans down and kisses my lips. "Behave while I am gone. I love you."

"Behave is my middle name." I give her an innocent look.

***

The morning has been uneventful. I have watched One Tree Hill—Team Naley all the way! Ate some cereal and flipped through social media on my phone, something I don't get much time to do on the farm.

I would be lying if I said I haven't missed it. The smell of the pastures, the animals talking, the sun rising. I know how blessed I have been to experience it. One day I hope Alyssa will love it too.

My phone rings and an unknown number pops up on caller ID.

At first, I think of ignoring it.

"Hello?" I answer.

"Is she not just beautiful? The way her skin feels against yours. The way her cunt is tight?"

I sit up nostrils flaring. "Kyle. How the fuck did you get my number?"

"You underestimate me, Cowboy." He lets out a deep chuckle.

I put him on speaker phone and text Cade: **THE FUCKER CALLED ME. UNKOWN NUMBER WHAT DO I DO?**

"No anger, Collin?" Kyle says when I don't respond.

Cade's text responds immediately: **I AM IN THE AREA. ON THE WAY. DO NOT PROVOKE HIM BUT KEEP HIM ON THE PHONE.**

"What do you want, Kyle?"

He hums, "My girl back."

Cade better hurry because I don't know how long I can hold back my anger. "Your girl?"

Kyle laughs again. "You really have no idea, do you? She is mine!"

Cade busts through the door of the apartment. I put my finger over my mouth for him to be quiet. I still have Kyle on speaker phone.

"Looks like you have company. I will be seeing you and my girl." Kyle lets out a sinful snarl before the line disconnects.

My eyes widen at Cade who darts out the door grabbing his radio yelling, "**I NEED ALL AVAILBLE UNITS AT SUNSET APARTMENTS IN CEDARVILLE. POSSIBLE 10-29.**"

"What is a 10-29?" I ask.

"Suspicious person," he answers from the front door looking out. "I didn't want to say stalker over the radio and there's not a 10 code for it. I don't know how smart this fucker is, and he could have a scanner for all we know."

"Cade. How is he getting away with all of this?"

He shrugs his shoulders. "Man, your guess is as good as mine. He is smart. Maybe ex-military or cop? He knows the laws."

"He kept saying, 'She is mine' Cade, what if he hurts her?" Adrenaline pumps through my veins.

Cade lets out a deep breath. "When does she get off?"

I look at the clock on the wall. "Twenty minutes or so."

He grabs his phone and calls someone. "Hey man. Need you to follow someone home from work."

I let out a breath, thankful for my friend and our community.

***

Alyssa

My shift was slow this morning. Most of our rush hours are at dinner time and lunch and I am thankful I am clocking out right before they begin.

I tell Lexie bye with a hug and head out the front door, stopping in my tracks when I notice a police cruiser sitting next to my car.

A man in a police uniform jumps out of the driver side giving me a soft smile. "Hello Miss. I have been ordered to follow you home."

"Wh-what? Why?"

He looks at me for a little longer than I am comfortable with. I guess he is trying to decide if I need to know the truth or a made-up lie.

"Cade said there was a disturbance at your apartment. He wanted me to make sure you got home safe."

My heart sinks. *Collin.*

I rush to my car, grabbing my keys from my purse without a second thought.

I pay no mind to the speed limit as I rush home, the police cruiser pulling out behind me.

My car halts suddenly in my parking space allowing me to run up to the door, pushing it open and seeing Cade and Collin sitting on the couch talking.

"Oh, thank god." I clutch my chest.

"What?" Cade says as the officer that followers me come up behind me.

"Next time, do not drive so fast." He flashes me a stern look.

I turn to face him. "I won't say sorry where this one is concerned," I point at Collin, "I will break every law."

Collin chuckles. "How about you don't do that."

I walk over to him, kissing him softly on the lips. "How about you tell me what happened here for me to have an escort home?"

He shares a look with Cade, making me nervous.

Chapter Twenty-Three
Alyssa

I feel bad for the mice now. The tiny creatures just trying to live a life when a big, scary, smart cat is stalking them.

That's what Kyle has made me feel like, a tiny mouse.

And that's where he gets off. Thinking he has control over not just my body, but my mind too.

At one point, he did.

But not anymore.

Collin holds my hand on the couch letting me process the news he and Cade gave me before Cade left with the other officers.

"He won't stop," I state.

Collin growls, "I think you need a day of relaxation."

My eyes dart to him. "How do I relax when he could be anywhere?"

He grabs me and pulls me into him, rubbing his hand over my shoulder and kisses my forehead. "I know the perfect place."

"Which is?"

He laughs. "Why don't we go visit the farm and my family tomorrow. You are off, and I don't have therapy. Doctors said it would be good for me to get out and try to walk some."

My eyes light up. I was just telling him the other day about how much I wanted to go and visit. Maybe ride a horse too.

"Really?" I smile at my cowboy.

"Of course! It will be good for the both of us."

***

The smell captivating me as I roll over in the bed makes my belly growl.

Feeling of the space beside me, I realize I am alone.

Sitting up, I grab my house coat and follow the smell into the kitchen. Collin stands in nothing but his black sweatpants.

If that was the only thing he wore for the rest of my life, I would be a happy girl.

"Sit down, pretty girl," he says without turning to face me. "I cooked you breakfast."

How did I ever make it without Collin Mapleson?

I do as I am told, walking over to the kitchen table, pulling out my chair and sitting down. He brings a plate over setting it in front of me. I drool at the sight before me: eggs, biscuits and gravy, and bacon.

"I love a man who can cook." I wink at him, and he bends, kissing me softly.

"And I love a woman who can eat."

I laugh. "Not cook?"

He walks back over to fix his plate. "Pretty girl. You leave the cooking to me. I don't want to die from food poisoning."

"Hey!" I bark at him, and he laughs.

I reach for the orange juice he already had on the table and pour me some into one of the empty drink glasses sitting beside it.

Taking a bite of my eggs, I close my eyes savoring the taste.

Every woman deserves to have a Collin Mapleson in her life.

Just not mine. I'll cut a bitch.

Collin stretches across the table to grab his phone. Swiping his fingers across the screen he holds it to his ear. "Megan? What's wrong?" a look of concern spreads over him.

I put my fork down, waiting on him to speak next.

Finally, he smiles making me relax. "Actually, Alyssa and I are getting out of the house for a little while today. Other than going to therapy and to get food, we don't get out much and the doctor says I am improving well." He winks at me before continuing. "I'm going stir crazy and the doctor said it would be good for me to walk around some. We are going to come by the farm and see everyone if you all will be home."

"Dinner?" Collin whispers to me.

I nod excitingly. "Ask her if I need to bring anything?"

He chuckles into the phone. "Will do. Be over soon."

He puts the phone down with a grin, "She said just to take care of me, and she would take care of the rest."

Finishing off my glass of orange juice I stand and make my way over to him. Pushing his plate back I sit down where it originally was in front of him.

His nostrils flare and his eyes darken. "I get dessert with breakfast?"

I bite my bottom lip before saying, "Best way I can think of to take care of you."

He grabs my legs, pushing them farther open and pushing me back with his hands so I am leaning on my elbows.

Running his hands up my thighs, he stops at the lace of my underwear. I am thanking the Lord above that I shaved last night.

"Come all over my face, madame." He winks at me before leaning in and running his fingers across the fabric of my panties making my eyes roll into the back of my head.

He pushes the cloth separating us to the side, exposing me. Blowing on me gently, my back arches from the sensation alone.

His tongue sweeps my flesh, tasting every inch of me.

"Collin," I moan.

"That's right baby. Say my name."

With one of my free hands, I grab a handful of his hair, massaging it with each lick he gives me.

"So good," I let out in between breaths.

His tongue penetrates me with a few thrusts, making me see stars. Removing his tongue, he inserts two fingers, making me cry out. His tongue goes to my clit, erotically circling the bundle of nerves building heat in my core.

Finding a rhythm with his fingers, he speeds up the movement of his tongue, allowing an eruption of euphoria to take me over.

"Fuck!" Every nerve in my body is tingling right now.

Chapter Twenty-Four
Collin

The **Magnolia Farm** sign comes into view when I turn into the driveway.

Alyssa fought me for the keys before I grabbed them from her and put them down my back side. She told me I didn't fight fair, and I assured her I needed to start back driving sometime. It was now or never.

"Oh, Collin. This place is beautiful." Her cheerful tone makes my heart flutter.

"It was my heaven on earth until I met you." I grab her hand with a squeeze.

She blushes and looks out her window at all the horses and cattle in the pasture.

Man, I have missed this place.

I won't lie though, maybe driving was not the best idea. My leg being bent for this long amount of time is starting to hurt a little.

I won't dare tell Alyssa that though.

Pulling her car up to the house, she jumps out before I even put the car in park.

"Can we explore today?" she asks, beaming at me coming around to my side.

She hands me my crutches from the backseat and helps me out. "Sure can." I give her a smile.

Seeing her so happy has my soul on fire. I always dreamed of sharing my love for this place with someone.

"Who is this?" Alyssa's baby voice catches me off guard as we reach the front porch. Reba, George, and Izzy meet us with tail wags and dancing butts.

I point to each telling her about them. And she bends down, giving each one pets.

Yep, that settles it. I will marry this woman.

She stops at the front door, unsure what to do next. "Go on in," I tell her.

"But that's not polite," she huffs.

"It's my house too, pretty girl." I laugh. "It's okay, I promise."

She grabs the handle of the screen door and steps inside but insists on saying, "Knock Knock," to whoever is inside.

I cannot help but laugh.

Before I make it inside fully, Megan is knocking the breath out of me with a giant bear hug. "Collin, I have missed you so much!" she exclaims.

I chuckle pointing at Alyssa who stands back letting us have our moment with a grin.

"This one has been taking good care of me, Meg. I think you would be pleased."

My eyes widen in shock when my sister does the last thing I ever expected, and apparently Alyssa, too, because she looks just as shocked when Megan throws her arms around her in a hug.

"Thank you for taking care of my baby brother," she tells her.

Alyssa nods but she doesn't blink.

"Make yourself at home," she tells Alyssa. "I need to go warm up Crackerjack this morning." She turns to me with a smile that almost touches her ears. "I qualified for nationals."

"I knew you would!" Gosh, I am so proud of her, and our grandparents would have been too.

"Y'all go, show Alyssa around the farm. I bet Maggie and Logan would love to see you too." I eye her, something seeming off, but she hurries out the door. "We will have supper here at the main house tonight."

And as fast as we stepped inside, she is gone to the barn.

"Odd, right?" Alyssa asks.

"She was too happy to be my sister. And she hugged you. She clearly has been cloned, and this new Megan wants to steal our farm."

Alyssa slaps my chest. "You are so dramatic. Come on, show me around, Cowboy."

Grabbing the keys to my truck, I throw them at Alyssa. "You drive."

She giggles. "Not ready for that, huh, big guy?"

"Just drive," I grumble.

She looks hot jumping up in the driver's side of my Chevy and turning the ignition. "Where to?" she asks, and I point to the road that leads past the barn and arena to the back side of the pasture where Logan and Maggie's house is.

"Just follow that road to the end."

"10-4," she salutes and pulls the shifter into drive.

I roll down my window when we pass the arena and wave at Megan who laughs and waves as we drive by. It even looks like Crackerjack bobs his head in acceptance.

***

"Can I get you anything to drink or eat?" Maggie asks us—mainly Alyssa—when we sit down in their living room.

"No, but thank you," Alyssa smiles at Maggie.

"I have to know," Logan starts, "How do you handle this goofball?"

I throw my arm around Alyssa and don't give her time to reply before I say, "Doggystyle is my favorite."

"Collin Mapleson!!" Maggie squeals but Logan laughs. It's Alyssa who makes me throw my head back into a laugh when she hides her face in her hands.

"Let me guess, not the first time he has said that?" Logan chuckles.

Alyssa sighs. "I am coming to realize I will never know what will come out of his mouth."

Rhett starts crying in another room and Maggie excuses herself to go get him.

"Well, you are the first girl he has brought home so I would bet you are special to him." He smiles at me.

"Someone wants to see you." Maggie states coming out with Rhett in her arms.

"Give me!!" I reach out to grab him from her and hold him gently against my chest on my forearm.

"Oh, he is adorable." Alyssa coos at him and his eyes are fixated on her.

"Easy killer. That's my woman; get your own." I joke.

Everyone in the room erupts in laughter.

"If you ever need a babysitter, you can call us," Alyssa offers, shocking even me.

"Oh, that would be wonderful." Maggie beams, "A date night or two would be great." She rubs Logan's shoulder. He gives her a wink.

"Are you sure?" I whisper to Alyssa.

She nods, "Of course. I love babies and your family is my family."

I lean down and kiss the top of her head. "You amaze me."

***

Before dinner, the last place I want to take Alyssa is the pond. It's the place Maggie and Logan got married and her dad—my uncle—built it, hoping she would return to the farm someday.

All four of us went swimming in it a few years ago when Maggie was Ivy, and we had no idea she was our long-lost cousin.

It's a long story and can be explained better through Maggie's point of view.

But the pond, it has always been one of my favorite places on the farm. After long hot days of working, I would come down here and cool off or Megan and I would swing from the rope hanging off the magnolia tree beside it.

I have never brought anyone I've dated to the farm, much less this pond. But Alyssa, it's one of the first places I wanted her to see.

Holding her hand walking across the pier that stretches across the water, I let her take in all the sounds, the colors, the animals.

The way the birds chirp off in the distance and the way the water moves with the slight breeze blowing.

"This is beautiful, Collin. All of it."

I smile, placing her in front of me, her back against my chest. I point to a spot of land across the distance. From the farmhouse it is to the right, but directly across from Maggie's house about 200 yards.

"Do you see that opening?"

She nods. "Yes, it would be a beautiful place to build a home."

I smile. Thankful I was patient. Thankful I waited to bring anyone else here but her. "It's mine."

She leans to the side, looking up at me, "Yours?"

"This farm is equally mine, Megan's, and Maggie's." I pause giving her time to process. "We run it together, and it was willed to all three of us. Each of us also has our own deeded plots of lands to use however we see fit."

"Oh, what a lovely legacy left to you all. Your grandparents must have been amazing people."

I choke down the tears forming. They were some of the best people I ever knew.

Taking a deep breath, I know the next question I ask, there is no coming back from.

"Alyssa, build a forever home with me out here on the farm."

She turns sharply to face me, her eyes widening. "Wh-what?"

I grab her hands. "I know we have only been dating a few months. I know this is fast and we don't have to do it right away, let me recover and we figure out what we are going to do about Kyle." I smile down at the beautiful woman before me.

"This has always been my home, Alyssa. It has been the place I always knew I was safe. But when I met you, you became my home, too. You became my priority. If you wanted me to give it all up, I would. We could stay in the apartment, and I would be happy because I would be with you." I pause searching her eyes. "But if a forever home on a slice of my heaven would be something you would consider; I want it with you."

A tear slides down her cheek making nerves scatter throughout my stomach.

It's too early. I have scared her. I just ruined everything.

"I want to share this heaven with you," she smiles, standing up on her tiptoes and kissing me deeply.

Chapter Twenty-Five
Alyssa

I am still overwhelmed with emotions as we make our way back to the barn for the evening. I had no idea when we arrived today that Collin would ask me about building a home with him.

Here on this farm.

It's one of the most beautiful places I have ever stepped foot on. The animals, the land, but most importantly, the family here. So much love is felt around, and I miss that part of my life.

When I lost my sister, home was not the same. A part of me left with her and I truly never thought I would get that back.

Until now.

Collin holds my hand as we walk into the barn, and I stop abruptly when I see Megan with her horse she called Crackerjack inside the barn. "That is a beautiful horse," I exclaim.

"Thank you," she smiles. "He is a brat sometimes."

"He is a brat all the time and you spoil him to where he thinks it's okay to act the way he does," Collin states.

Crackerjack pins his ears at him and Megan and I both laugh.

"He takes care of me, Collin. He deserves pampering," Megan huffs.

I slowly make my way around the barn, taking time to look at each horse in its stall. A brown colored one sticks his head out of the stall window when I get close and nuzzles into me, making me giggle.

"You want to ride him?" Maggie asks with Logan not far behind her, Rhett in his arms. I notice Maggie is still getting around slowly from surgery and Logan helps her keep her balance.

"Oh, no. It's okay." Honestly, I want to. They just terrify me.

Maggie gives me a sincere, knowing grin and heads over to Tiny's stall beside me.

"He is the best boy. Took care of me when I first arrived. I promise he will take care of you." She rubs Tiny's nose, and he lays his head over on her.

"You were just saying the other day how you wished you had horses growing up," Collin admits.

Thanks for the backup.

I roll my eyes at him, but honestly what's the point of getting on with my life if I don't face my fears?

Megan puts Crackerjack back in his stall after hosing him down from their ride and grabs a halter, walking into Tiny's stall to get him out.

My heart falls to my feet.

I can't believe I am doing this.

Megan throws a few loops around the stall wall. Heading inside the tack room, she comes out with a brush and brushes Tiny's back before throwing a pad over his back.

We all look up when a sound is heard in the distance—it sounds like a four-wheeler or atv.

"Logan, will you go flag down Derek and tell him a horse is out here. He can park it outside the barn until we are done," Megan asks.

Logan nods, walking with Rhett still in his arms outside the barn.

Before we know it, the Ranger is flying past a yelling Logan, into the barn, and Tiny jumps back tearing off out of the barn.

Thankfully, he must have not gone far because Megan runs out the barn and comes back in no time holding the end of his lead walking him back inside.

Logan hands Rhett over to Maggie and gets in Derek's face. "What the fuck dude!"

"What?" Derek asks.

"I was trying to get you stop because we have a horse out in the barn." He points at Maggie and Rhett. "You better be thankful neither of them are hurt. So, help me God, I would end you."

"I just thought you was coming to give me shit for what I did to Megan last night."

Logan grabs his arm, and Collin hops on his crutches over to him giving him a death glare. "What the fuck did you do Megan?" we all ask in unison—well besides Megan, who looks embarrassed.

Logan steps towards Derek. "I won't ask again."

Derek forces Logan's arm off him. "I don't have to tell you shit. You still have your wife and son. You don't have any idea what the hell I have been through. I'm out of here."

Derek gives me a look and my heart breaks for him. He has let the darkness consume him more than I have.

"Just let him go," I tell the men. "This is how he deals with his emotions. He leaves. He has been through a lot."

By the way Megan is staring at me, I know I will have to bring up the past soon.

***

I hope they cannot tell I am literally shaking in my boots.

Megan gave me a pair of hers to put on and we brought Tiny out to the arena once Megan saddled him for me.

"You look beautiful," Collin whispers behind me, leaning on his crutches.

"How do I get up there?" I ask, looking up at the giant before me. Tiny didn't look this tall in his stall.

"The same way you mount me," Collin winks and Megan gags.

"What is wrong?" Maggie asks, walking up with Logan and Rhett.

"Collin is being Collin," Megan snarls.

I am mortified. "Anyway, I can get a muzzle for him?" I ask Megan.

She laughs. "If it was possible I would have done it a long time ago." She pulls on the stirrup, "Put your left foot in and swing over."

I force down the lump in my throat and do as I am told.

"Whoa." I squeal once in the saddle. It's higher than I thought it would be. Tiny sways under me, making me tense up.

"You are okay," Collin assures me. "He is just getting flies off his feet."

I nod. "Okay, now what?"

Megan throws the reins over Tiny's neck and hands them to me. "Now you ride your first horse."

The feeling of this animal under me is unlike anything I ever thought it would be. I can feel his power with every move, but he is gentle.

"Barely nudge him in the sides to walk," Collin tells me, and I do as I am told. Tiny steadily walks around the arena, my body moving with him.

"This is so cool!" I yell back at the group.

Facing my fear has never been more freeing; it has given me wings to live.

I lean down and pat Tiny's neck. "You are a good boy, aren't you?"

***

We all went to the front porch while we waited on dinner to finish cooking—minus Megan; she is the one doing the cooking.

While Maggie and Logan catch up with Collin, I make my way inside to see if I can help with anything.

"Can I help you?" I ask Megan once the door shuts behind me.

She stands beside the kitchen table with plates in her hand. It's her eyes that get my full attention; she looks sad.

"Megan," I sigh, "He is not a bad guy. He has just been delt a rough deck of cards is all."

She doesn't look at me. "How do you know Derek?"

The questions hits me like a ton of bricks knocking the air from my lungs. I can feel the tears starting to form. "I am assuming since he has been so upset lately, he's told you about Haley?"

She nods but doesn't offer to speak.

I guess today is all about facing fears.

"Haley meant a lot to both of us," I start. "She was my twin sister."

Megan sweeps in with a hug, making the tears fall even more. "I am so sorry," she whispers.

"I am not excusing his behavior by no means," I pause, taking a few deep breaths. "Because lord knows, he has a temper. But he is lost. I could always go home and hang out with friends to get away from the grief. He went home to an empty bed, Megan. He went home to memories of her. He lost everything he thought his future was going to be. I could not imagine coming home and not having Collin there after having him with me so much these past few weeks."

"I am Haley's sister and losing her was hard enough; I cannot imagine how it feels being her husband." I wipe my tears. "Losing their home too was even worse. All those memories just vanished with her. The pictures, the memorabilia, the souvenirs from vacations, all gone. One mistake cost him everything and it haunts him with every breath he takes."

The next words out of her mouth, shock me. "He took me to meet her. He took me to Haley's grave."

I rub her shoulder, "He must really care for you then. For the longest time, he wouldn't allow anyone but himself to go out and visit her gravesite . . .. Sounds like he found a light in you, and something scared him off."

I search her eyes, and she nods.

"I told him I qualified for Nationals, and he blew up in my face. He kicked me out of bed."

I huff, not shocked in the least. This is what he does. "Sounds like something he would do," I tell her. "He is afraid of people he cares about leaving again. It's a survival mode he has put himself into. As far as I know, you are the only one he has been with since Haley."

She straightens up and picks up the plates again, setting the table. "Yeah, well that's the second time he has kicked me out of the bed, and I'll be damned if it happens again."

I chuckle. "Make him grovel for it."

Megan laughs. "Thank you for being good to my brother. I am sorry I was mean when we first met."

My smile turns soft, thankful for this talk we just had. "Don't be sorry. I would be worried if you didn't give me a tough time."

*****

"Oh my gosh. Not sweet Maggie!" I laugh.

Sitting around the dinner table with Collin's family has brought back a spark in my soul I thought was lost forever. I remember sitting with my parents, Haley, and Derek just like this.

I hope he figures out how stupid he is being and quick. The Mapleson kids sure are a family everyone would be lucky to be included in.

"Sweet my ass," Logan says, and Maggie hits him over the head.

Laughter breaks out again amongst the cousins.

"Think we need to fire Derek." Logan changes the subject quickly.

"Logan." Megan sighs. "It's okay, we aren't going to do that."

"He clearly did something you don't want to tell us about." He looks at Megan sternly and it makes my stomach sink for her.

Maggie puts her hands on Logan's shoulders. "Logan, I understand you're concerned. We all are. But she is a big girl and can handle herself."

"Well, I agree with Logan," Collin chimes in.

I place my hand on his knee, and he looks at me concerned.

"I know I am an outsider here," I start, "but if I may, Derek has been through a lot more than he lets on. He lashes out when he is afraid of his emotions." I pause, taking a deep breath and look around the table at everyone. "I know Derek because he was married to my sister. He lost her and their home to a house fire he caused by accident. She was also twenty-eight weeks pregnant."

Maggie and Logan's eyes widen. "He has been through a lot. We all have. I am not excusing him, but I do know he comes with a lot of baggage," I tell them, picking up my drink to take a sip when I finish.

Maggie reaches up, wiping a tear from her eye. "That's what he meant by you still had me and our son. Logan, I couldn't imagine if we were in his shoes."

Logan clears his throat. "He better not try that shit again." He stands abruptly, walking with Maggie into the den where Rhett lays taking a nap.

"Why have you never told me he was married to Haley?" Collin grabs my hand.

It's not that I didn't want to tell him. It's just I didn't know how and I had enough on my plate with Kyle.

I shrug. "Not my story to tell. I am only going to bat for him for my sister's sake. I promised her I would go to bat for him. She would want someone fighting for him."

Collin pulls me in kissing me softly. Today has been a day full of therapy that I had no idea I needed.

Chapter Twenty-Six
Collin

Alyssa drives us down the driveway back to the apartment after a wonderful day with my family. It has refueled my soul being back on the farm with them today.

"Thank you for today." I grab her hand and place it in my lap.

She smiles. "Thank you for sharing today with me and getting me out of the house. I would have driven myself insane wondering where Kyle was."

I want to share every day with her, every good day, bad day, and all the days in between. I want them with her.

"Also, I think you might have some competition." She winks at me.

I raise an eyebrow, "Really? Let me guess, it has four legs and a cute face?"

She giggles. "Well, I was going to say Rhett, but yes, Tiny is a close second."

My eyes twinkle at the memory of Rhett cooing at her. We have never really discussed the idea of kids someday, though after today, I would be willing to put a baby in her tonight.

"You think of having that someday?" I ask.

She takes her eyes off the road to look at me for a brief second before returning them forward. "Um, yeah. I guess. I was never someone who wanted a house full but one or two would make me happy. Especially after watching you, your sister, and cousin. I would want my child to have that someday."

I squeeze her hand. "Our child."

"You would want to have babies with me, Collin Mapleson?" Her tone is playful.

"Let's get home and we can practice." I lean in kissing her neck. "How about when they are a little older and ask how they came into this world I can tell them doggy style."

She gasps making me chuckle; I knew that would get a rise from her.

"Second thought. Kids can wait," she jokes.

I lean over the middle console that is separating us and rest my hand on her upper thigh. "You sure? Practicing would be fun." I run my hand over the button of her pants slowly unbuttoning them.

Her mouth falls open. "Collin," she breathes out when my hand slowly slips inside her panties.

"Watch the road," I whisper into her ear, dropping my lips to her neck and place a small bite over her carotid artery. The vein starts to pump erotically against my lips.

My fingers pull back the cloth of her panties, allowing me access to her flesh. A primal growl leaves me when I realize she is soaked.

"Naughty girl," I whisper. "You are so wet for me."

She picks her hips up making me smirk. My pretty girl is allowing me more access.

I run my greedy fingers over her clit and her head tilts back. "Watch the road," I remind her.

"It's so sensitive," she mumbles.

"Let's see just how sensitive," I tell her and stick a finger inside. She gasps but does well to focus on driving while traffic passes by us.

"Collin, I swear I can't make it. I need to pull over," she whispers through moans while I thrust another finger in.

"You want my cock don't you pretty girl?" I purr.

"Ye-yes," she moans out and pulls the car into an empty parking lot. Throwing the car in park, she shocks me by climbing out of her seat and straddling me.

Grabbing her chin, I pull her in to kiss me deeply. Her tongue sweeps in dancing with mine and I think I might explode right here from her kiss alone.

"I need these pants gone," she snarls picking her body off me and pulling her pants as far down her thighs as she can. "Pick yourself up," she orders, and I don't argue.

Her needy hands unbuckle my jeans and free my cock in one swift move. I like seeing her confident and not afraid. She has come such a long way, and I couldn't be prouder of her becoming herself again.

"Sit on my cock pretty girl," I order her, and she impales herself in one movement, making us both gasp from the sensation.

Our lips crash together again, gasping for air every few seconds while she rides me with a rhythm I never want to stop.

"I. Am. So. Sensitive," she moans, and I notice it too. Whatever is causing it, I don't want it to stop, it has turned my girl into a wild animal.

Reaching down, my thumb rubs circular motions around her clit taking no time for her insides to clamp down around my cock, our eruptions pouring into one another.

We don't move, staying connected while we catch our breaths, our foreheads resting on each other. "I love you," I tell her.

She kisses my forehead. "I love you, Collin."

"Doggy style later?" I joke—kinda.

"I might just take you up on that." She kisses my forehead.

"Booyah!!" I fist pump the air.

Chapter Twenty-Seven
Alyssa

I wake up sore the next morning, most likely from the way I was straddling Collin in the car last night—or the doggy style he put me into when we came home last night.

My cowboy lays beside me snoring so I carefully ease myself out of bed to the bathroom. I don't know what it has been lately, but I pee more during the day, no matter how much—or little—I drink.

When my feet hit the ground, I must sprint to the bathroom and barely make it before I am puking in the toilet.

"Alyssa?" Collin's worried voice is heard from the bedroom. It doesn't take him long to hop into the bathroom looking at me with big eyes.

"You think you caught a bug?" he asks me while reaching for a washcloth from the closet and wetting it.

I puke again. The taste is burning my throat. "Ugh. I don't know but this is awful."

"Here." He hands me the washcloth.

I run over my mind of the possible reasons I may be sick, and my eyes widen.

Oh. My. God.

"Collin. What is today's date?" I ask trying not to panic.

He hops back to the bedroom and come back in with his phone. "The fourteenth."

I think I might pass out now. Grabbing the side of the vanity, I steady myself.

"Hand me my phone." I try to remain calm.

He goes back into the bedroom and comes back with my phone handing it to me. "Everything okay?"

Ignoring him I pull up Lexie's number and hit dial.

"Hey girl!" she answers chipper.

"I need you to do me a favor."

"Anything. I am off today."

Taking a deep breath, my eyes hold Collin's. "Run to the market and grab me a pregnancy test."

Bang.

Collin is laying on the floor completely limp.

"And Cade, too. Collin just passed out." I try not to laugh.

"Are you serious!! Oh my gosh! On our way!" she pauses. "Make sure he is breathing!"

I laugh. "He is. Poor guy may have a headache when he gets up."

We hang up the phone and I bend down checking on my guy. His eyes flutter while he comes back to reality. He looks up at me with wide eyes. "Is it really possible?"

I nod. "Well, we do have a lot of unprotected sex and if the date's right, I am late by a few weeks."

His head falls back on the floor. "I am terrified," he says honestly.

"Passing out might have given that away," I joke.

"It's not that I wouldn't be happy. I would. We talked about this last night. It's just, with everything that is going on with Kyle, I don't want anything happening to you." His hand goes to my belly, "Or our baby."

Tears crease my eyes; he doesn't even know if it's for sure yet and he is happy about it. We have only been dating a few months and this is awful timing, but he is still happy about it.

Once I help him up and we make it to the living room, I try to diffuse his worry by saying. "Please do not tell our kid they were conceived doggy style."

He laughs. "Only if it's a boy."

"Collin," I warn. "Don't."

He wraps his arms around me. "I am kidding."

I would be telling a lie if I said I wasn't nervous but the more I think about it—I would be shocked if the test was negative. Last night I was so sensitive, more than normal. I have been peeing more lately and then I got sick this morning.

Cade and Lexie are knocking on the front door thirty minutes later and when I open it, a shit eating grin is all over her face.

"Glad you are alive, brother," Cade jokes stepping inside and taking a seat beside Collin.

"I will definitely have a sore head tomorrow," Collin winces.

Lexie follows me into the bathroom and shuts the door behind me.

"Privacy?" I ask her.

She waves me off, taking a seat on the vanity counter. "What's that?"

I giggle. "Okay. But don't you dare scream if its two lines."

She does a happy dance. "It totally is going to be positive. I can feel it in my bones."

I take the test out of the box and set them both on the counter beside the toilet. "Hand me one of those mouthwash cups." I point to the sink and Lexie turns around grabbing it and hands it to me.

Dropping my pants, I pee in the cup and set it down on the counter beside the test

After pulling my pajama pants up, I reach for the test and take the top off, stick it into the cup and pull it back out, then place the cap back on.

"Three minutes," I say, turning my back, not wanting to watch.

Lexie's eyes widen. "How late did you say you were?"

"A few weeks. Why?" The look on her face is worrying me.

"Because babe. You don't need the full three minutes. Those lines are dark!"

I jump back around to the counter, my eyes finding the test. Sure enough, two dark lines have appeared confirming my suspicion.

Lexie screams, "You are pregnant!!"

A few seconds later, Cade yells, "Collin's passed out again."

***

"Are you sure you are, okay?" I ask Collin in the room of the OB-GYN clinic.

He came back to quickly after Lexie and I rushed out into the living room. He heard her scream and went out cold again. I am starting to think he may not make it in the delivery room.

We decided to call my gynecologist, and they were able to get me in within an hour. The nurse just left the room and Collin's leg is bouncing ninety miles an hour beside me.

I almost dreamed about the day I would find out I was pregnant. But no one ever prepared me for how calm I would be seeing those lines on the test.

The fear I had felt when I turned my back to the test was consuming me. But the moment I turned back around and my reality hit, a surprising wave of calm crashed through me.

This baby was mine. And I will always protect what's mine.

I would be lying if I said I wasn't sad that my sister wasn't here. What I would give to be able to call her right now and cry tears of happiness together.

"I am fine." Collin grabs my hand. He is trying to put on a brave face, but deep down I know he is scared too.

"Good morning." A young girl comes in wheeling an ultrasound machine.

"Hey." I smile at her.

"Let me get you to lay back on the table. We are going to see if we can get a heartbeat."

Collin stands beside me, holding my hand while she sets everything up.

"This may be cold for a minute," she tells me, squirting liquid on my stomach and gliding a device over my skin.

A few seconds later, the most beautiful sound hits my ears.

Our baby's heartbeat.

"That's a strong heart." The woman smiles at me. "If you look at the screen here," she points to the computer on her machine, "You can see your sweet little peanut."

She clicks some buttons, taking pictures, and stands. "Everything looks great. I am going to let the doctor come in now and discuss things with you." She smiles and exits.

I hear a sniffle beside me and look over at Collin. Crocodile tears flood his cheeks.

"Collin?" I question him.

"These are happy tears," he assures me. "That is our baby, pretty girl."

"You are going to be a daddy." I fight back my own tears.

"I love you so much." He kisses my lips softly. "You and our little family."

Chapter Twenty-Eight
Collin

Something changed the moment I heard that heartbeat.

My grandfather's words ring truer now than before. *You won't truly become a man until you hear your child's heartbeat for the first time.*

They say, *grown men don't cry;* but I disagree.

I believe real men do cry and those tears are the overflow of love their heart gains when they have their own *home.*

I don't mean home in the physical sense. I mean home as in the family you create. The love it takes to make a child. The love it takes to protect what is yours. The love you unlock when you find your forever.

When a grown man cries, it symbolizes rebirth. The little boy is gone, and the man has arrived.

Life as I know it has changed forever, and I couldn't be happier.

I open the door of the apartment and allow Alyssa to walk inside first. Thankfully, I am starting to get around good on my leg and hopefully after my next follow up next week, I will be cleared from the crutches for good.

"Aw. Look!" Alyssa squeals, Lexie and Cade must have brought over flowers.

I notice them around the same time she does. A dozen white roses sit on the kitchen table.

"I thought you took removed the key you hid on the porch?" I ask her confused how they got in here.

"I did. But I gave the key to Lexie in case I ever needed her to get inside. You can never be too careful when there is a psycho on the loose." She smirks at me.

"Speaking of psycho." I start. "He has been quiet again lately. Cade said there has been no unusual activity and no new updates."

Alyssa sets her vitamins the doctor instructed us to get down on the kitchen counter and grabs a water from the fridge. "Hopefully he got the hint and left."

She takes out her vitamins and pops a few in her mouth, washing them down with the water.

I shake my head. "No, I am not putting my guard down that easy. Not when I have you and our baby to protect."

She sits her water bottle down and walks over to me, wrapping her arms around me. "We are so lucky to have you, daddy."

I grin. "Daddy? Are you calling me that or is the baby?"

I get my confirmation when her hand cups my cock. "What do you think?"

"I think Daddy is ready to play." I wink scooping her in my arms and walking her to the bedroom.

Laying her gently down on the mattress, my hands pull up the bottom of her shirt and I kiss her belly. "Close your eyes and ears little one. It's adult time."

Alyssa giggles. "Collin!"

"What?" I laugh. "I am just making sure he or she doesn't get any bad first impressions of me."

Pulling her shirt over her head, I toss it to the floor and start unbuttoning her pants. My girl looks gorgeous laying before me in her bra and panties.

Her legs land off the bed and I pull them further apart. Her wetness glistening on the fabric of her panties makes my cock twitch.

"You are ready for me pretty girl," I tell her, and she blushes.

"Doctor said the blood flow from pregnancy will make me more sensitive."

In record time, I remove my clothes and stand in front of her, my dick begging to be inside her. Pulling her legs closer to the edge of the mattress gets me closer to her entrance and I run the head of my cock through her wetness. The sensation makes me see stars.

"Hang on. I am going in." I wink at her and with one violent push, I feel her flesh tighten all around me.

Pulling out and pushing back in, I stretch her with my length making her back arch. "Collin," she moans. "Oh my god. Collin!!"

"That's Daddy Collin to you!" I joke and she grins.

Picking her legs up, I place them over my shoulders giving me access to all of her. "You are so beautiful," I tell her as I pick up my pace.

Reaching for her clit, I pinch the bundle of nerves that I know always makes her erupt. Being more sensitive like she has been lately; I am sure this will send her into another universe.

"Ahhh!!!" Her orgasm rips through her, and her pussy clamps down on me, making me lose my vision as my own orgasm rushes from me.

"Oh my god! Your leg!" Alyssa says after a moment of coming off her high.

I forgot about it, too. In the heat of the moment, I didn't realize I have been standing here, my body weight on both feet.

After I pull out of her, Alyssa jumps off the bed, her own legs a little wobbly after what we just did, and she inspects my leg.

"How does it feel?" she asks.

"Honestly, never better." I grin. And I meant it.

This has been the best day.

***

ALYSSA

Lexie and Cade's knock on the front door startles me as I am pulling plates down from the cabinets. She called me shortly after our activities in the bedroom and wanted to bring pizza and come hang out with us tonight.

"She has a key, doesn't she?" Collin asks from the bathroom.

"Supposed to," I state, walking over to the door and check in the peep hole to make sure it is them.

It is. Lexie has a big grin on her face when I open the door.

"Don't you have a key?" I question her.

She looks at me confused. "No? I mean, I did but I gave it back to you. Remember?"

"No?" I question her. "When was this?"

She pulls out her phone and holds up her text messages. "I got a text from you wanting it back. You told me I could just leave it back under the plant it originally stayed under out front, and you would get it."

My eyes widen. I race to grab my phone from the kitchen counter and pull up our conversations. My phone doesn't have any of those messages.

"I didn't text you." I tell her and my eyes go to Cade's.

He pushes us all inside the apartment and shuts the door, locking it behind him.

"When were those messages sent?" he asks Lexie, and she hands him her phone.

Collin comes out of the bathroom and looks at us confused. "What is going on?"

My eyes notice the flowers in the background beside him and my heart rate accelerates. "Lexie . . . did you put those roses on the kitchen table for me?"

The look on her face is all I need to know but she shakes her head. "No, Alyssa. I haven't been inside here without you other than when we cleaned for you."

"Are you telling me that mother fucker has been inside this apartment!?" Collin yells.

Cade pulls his phone to his ear and says, "Hey Charlie. Can you run some checks on a phone. See where these messages originated from."

He nods as the other person talks and gives them the information they need. "Thanks, man. Call me soon as you get a hit."

He pockets his phone and his eyes reach Collins. "If we can ping him, I will be able to arrest him for questioning."

Collin snarls, "This fucker needs to be dealt with." He wraps his arms around me, his hold tightening around me. I feel his worry without him saying a word.

Chapter Twenty-Nine
Collin

Cade advised us last night to stay home today. He hopes he will be able to find Kyle and bring him in for questioning.

The security cameras had been cut remotely the day those messages were sent to Lexie, so we were not able to get video of him sneaking inside.

My blood boils through my veins just thinking of him having a way to get inside.

"I need to change the locks." I tell Alyssa while we sit at the kitchen table eating breakfast.

She sighs. "Already thought about that. The owner of the apartment complex refuses to give me permission to do so."

I snarl. "Did you tell him what was going on?"

She nods. "Yeah. He said he doesn't have the budget for it and all the keys have to be the same. So, if he changes ours, he has to change everyone else's."

That prick.

"We could go to the farm this week until Cade finds something. You would be safe there."

She looks at me fighting back her tears. "I am tired of running. I am tired of being afraid. I will regret it if I run. I need to stand up to him."

I watch her take a bite of her food. She is calm this morning. Actually, she has been calm since the morning she took that pregnancy test. The once fearful, weak woman I met on a random weekday has turned into a fierce mama bear ready to hunt down anyone who tries to harm her family.

"Promise me you will keep your gun close."

She nods. "I promise. I cannot stay here all week. I need to work; we will have so many things to pay for in the coming months."

"I am not worried about that," I assure her. "The farm makes enough money for us to live off of."

"But I am. I will go crazy sitting at home all day letting my mind wander," she says honestly.

I smile. She continues to amaze me every day.

"Okay, but let's not think about it right now. Let's just relax today." I stand, grabbing my plate and hers and walking into the kitchen to clean up the mess I made cooking.

***

CADE

"I got it from here, Charlie," I tell my coworker as I step into the interrogation room.

It didn't take us long to find him. The dumbass covered all his tracks but what he didn't cover was the router he used to send the messages and hack Alyssa's phone.

I got a phone call this morning before my alarm went off and came on in once I gave the okay for my fellow deputies to bring him in.

Honestly, I'm afraid I won't have anything to hold him on and the fucker knows that as he sits there grinning at me. While we could find the messages he sent pretending to be Alyssa, there was no trace of him cutting the cameras at the apartment.

The fucker is smart.

I deal with dumbasses like him all day long and I swear, I don't get paid enough for the job I do. But for my friends, I will gladly wake up at the ass crack of dawn to put the fear of God in this son of a bitch.

Sitting my coffee down, I take a seat and eye Kyle for a few minutes. His eyes dance back at me, a hint of the devil in them.

"Let's get this over with." He smiles.

"Got places to be?" I ask.

'Something like that."

I haven't told Collin we brought him in yet. I wanted to question him first and get a feel for how he reacts.

"Tell me why you're here." I lean back in my chair.

He shrugs. "I guess you hero types want something to pin on me."

That's not the answer I was expecting. "Pin something on you? Like what?"

He leans into the table. "You tell me, officer."

"Well, from the intel I was given this morning, you were pretending to be someone else by hacking their phone and texting like you were them. Is that right?"

His grin grows. "She a friend of yours, huh?"

"Who?" I cock an eyebrow.

"My girl. Beautiful, isn't she?"

"What's her name," I coax him.

"Alyssa."

I grab my coffee, taking a sip. "Why don't you tell me why you think she is yours."

He chuckles. "Because she needed someone like me in her life. She was mine from the moment we met. She told me when I would ask her."

"Is that why you won't leave her alone?" I test him.

His eyes turn dark. "I don't know what you are talking about."

"I think you do," I assure him.

"I think you are asking me questions outside of why you have me in here. Which is nothing to hold me." His smile returns. "So, Mr. Officer, when do I get to go?"

This fucker is starting to piss me off.

***

Collin

My phone rings once I push the start button on the dishwasher.

"Hey Cade," I answer.

His voice on the other end sounds exhausted. "Man, I have some bad news."

I put him on speaker phone and walk over to Alyssa on the couch. "I have you on speaker so Alyssa can hear you."

He takes a big inhale of air and releases it slowly. "I've had Kyle in my interrogation room all morning."

Alyssa's eyes widen at me, and I reach for her hand, holding it tightly.

"And?" I ask.

"He is smart, Collin. He knew when to shut up and get around my questions. He knows the law. Alyssa, does he have any ex-police or military training?"

She shakes her head. "Not that I am aware of."

"He has done his research for sure. And he swears you are his. He kept telling me that. Said you told him."

Alyssa's worried eyes hold mine before she yells. "He is a fucking liar. Yes, I did tell him that, but it was only to calm him down when he would get abusive or when I didn't want him to hit me."

I rub my hand over hers. "Shh. Don't get worked up. It's not good for you or the baby."

"I'm sorry guys. I had no reason to keep him. My superior made me let him leave."

"What?" Alyssa squeals.

"Cade, what do we need to do?" I ask him.

"Stay low. Don't leave unless together. Alyssa, keep your gun on you. And get your own cameras up. You can get ones that work on WIFI and connect to your phone. I will continue working on my end and please call me if there are any issues." He sighs. "I wish there was more I could do."

Alyssa fights back tears. "No, thank you for all you have done. We appreciate you and your friendship."

"Thanks man." I tell him too before we hang up.

"He is not going to win," she says sternly. "As God is my witness, he will be six feet under by the time I am done with him."

I pull her into me, "Easy now killer. I don't need my baby mama behind bars."

She chuckles. "Don't think I would be cute with a baby bump wearing an orange jump suit?"

I kiss her forehead and laugh. "You would be the most beautiful orange pumpkin I ever did see."

I knew that would get a hand slap to my chest.

Chapter Thirty
Alyssa

It has been a week since Cade called to tell us about Kyle's questioning.

And it's time for me to go back to work. I cannot sit here and do nothing while he is off laughing somewhere, knowing he has altered my life.

He hasn't and that is not an example I want to give my child.

Running away from their problems only causes unwanted stress, fear, and anxiety.

I refuse to live in a world full of that. I want to be able to enjoy this pregnancy without fear of his next move.

He stole enough from me; it's time I take my life back.

It's barely six o clock in the morning; my shift starts at eight. Thankfully, I have not had much morning sickness since the morning I found out I was pregnant, but I am afraid to get my hopes up.

Collin is still snoozing in the bed, so I ease into the bathroom and remove my pajamas to get a shower.

Pulling back the curtains, I turn the water off and smile when I see my sleepy cowboy leaned up against the door frame watching me.

"I have a feeling you like me, Mr. Mapleson," I smirk.

He pushes off the post and walks into the bathroom, handing me my towel and wrapping it around me. Leaning down, he presses a kiss to my forehead. "Maybe a little."

Walking back to the sink, he grabs his toothbrush and starts brushing his teeth.

"You sure you will be okay going by yourself?" I ask him.

He has his last follow-up today with the surgeon and because I am scheduled to work this morning, we will be departing our own ways.

"Yes," he says after rinsing his mouth. "I will swing by the restaurant afterward and have lunch with you," he assures me. "Keep your gun with you. Just in case," he tells me.

"I will." I rub my belly, "We will be fine, Daddy."

He grabs me, pulling my towel to bring me closer to him and places a soft kiss on my lips. My body reacts before my mind catches up and a short moan leaves me.

"Careful, darling. We don't need to be late." But his kiss deepens into mine and his hand runs up under my towel, his fingers tracing circles over my clit.

I pull him harder into me, not able to get close enough to him.

"Is that what you want?" he whispers.

"Yes." I moan when he moves his fingers from my clit and sticks one inside me.

"Always so wet for me," he growls.

He pulls his finger out and when he goes in again, he adds two more. Three of his fingers pump in and out of me, making heat swell in my core.

Before I can stop myself, I let my towel drop to the floor and grab his boxers, pulling them down.

"Well, look at my girl being so confident," he says proudly.

In one swift move, he picks me up under my ass and lifts me, allowing my legs to drape around him. He walks me to the bathroom vanity, sitting me down on the edge of it, his cock lining up with my entrance.

"Is this what you want, Madame?" he winks.

But instead of answering, I pull him into me with a fierce kiss tying our tongues together in a heat of passion.

In one graceful thrust, he is inside me making us both moan out, the sensation taking us over.

"You drive me crazy with this perfect pussy," he whispers when our kiss breaks and his lips go to my neck, sucking and biting.

"Collin. Oh. My God. Collin," I yell out when the pleasure builds to the point of release making me clamp down around him.

The warmth of his seed spills over into me making me see stars as endorphins scatter through my brain.

***

Collin left shortly after seven to get to his appointment. Lexie is coming to pick me up since she works the same shift I do. We plan to pick up Collin's truck this evening from the farm once I get off work.

Honestly, I feel like after my lease is up, we may move back full time. Collin misses it out there and I have nothing keeping me here.

My phone rings, getting my attention. "Hey mom." I smile. I haven't spoken to my parents in weeks since they have been off on their trip.

"Honey. How are you?"

My eyes widen. They don't know they have a grandbaby on the way.

"I am good. Are you guys back yet?"

I can feel my mom grinning on the other end. "Our last flight leaves in an hour then we are home. I just wanted to check on you. It made me worry when we finally got phone service and I didn't have a single call or text from you."

I smile. "I am good mom. Let me know when your back home. Collin and I would love to have dinner with you and dad soon."

"We would love that dear. It's been too long."

A tear creases my eyes. It has.

"Got to go. Call you soon," she says, and we hang up.

Heading back into the bathroom, I grab my makeup bag and start applying my makeup for the day.

Grabbing my mascara, I unscrew the cap before lifting it to my eye. An unwanted sneeze sneaks up on me making me fling the mascara into the sink, averting my eyes from the mirror I was just looking in.

When my eyes come back to the mirror, I gasp.

"Miss me, sugar?"

"Kyle." I try to remain calm. "What are you doing here?"

He chuckles grabbing me by my hair and dragging me into the hallway. "What am I doing here? I am here to collect what's mine."

"I am not yours!" I scream and kick him in the thigh giving me time to bolt down the hall into the living room.

I almost make it to my purse before my body falls to the ground. The son of a bitch has knocked my legs out from under me.

"Kyle! Stop!" I scream but he is too strong, pulling me back to him.

My nails dig into the carpet, trying to keep myself from moving toward him but he is so much stronger than I am.

My phone has to be close, so I yell, "Siri! Call Collin Mapleson!"

The phone starts ringing in the background giving me an advantage to get away as it grabs Kyle's attention.

"Hey pretty girl." Collin answers and I scream. "Collin! Kyle's here! Collin! Help!"

"He won't get here in time before I get what I came here for," Kyle snarls at me.

"You son of a bitch. Don't you fucking touch her!" Collin yells on the other end before Kyle walks over to my phone and disconnects the call.

"You won't be needing this anymore." He throws the phone up against the wall.

Tears crease my eyes. "Kyle, stop."

In three steps, he is back at me, grabbing my hair and pulling me down on the floor. "Kyle stop!" I say again. "I'm pregnant."

That doesn't seem to faze him. "I know." His evil laugh rings out. "Didn't you get my flowers of congratulations? It's okay. I'll forgive you once I get rid of it."

My eyes widen. "No! Get your fucking hands off me!"

I scratch at him, clawing at his eyes, nose, and face. "You fucking bitch!"

He jumps off me grabbing his eyes giving me enough momentum to crawl backwards grabbing my purse.

"Come here! I don't remember you being so fucking insane," he growls.

My hand reaches inside my purse, making him stop in his tracks when the barrel of my pistol is pointing back at him.

His hands hold up in surrender. "Whoa. Put that down."

"No." I cry. "You have stolen too much from me."

"You are mine," he sneers.

I huff, rolling my eyes. "I am not fucking yours. But you know what is mine? This baby. And the worst fucking thing you ever did was threaten to get rid of it."

I click the safety off the way Collin showed me. "All the shit you did to me. Raping me. Mentally and physically abusing me. Stalking me." I pause. "I was once a naïve little girl who was weak. I let you have power over me."

Placing my finger on the trigger, I smile. "Meet the new me. A mama bear who will do whatever it takes to protect what's mine."

The sound of the gun rings out over the apartment and Kyles lifeless body falls to the floor.

Chapter Thirty-One
Collin

I shouldn't have left her alone.

The thought runs through my mind when the phone disconnects. My appointment could have been rescheduled, or I could have just cancelled it.

The blood pumping through my veins sends a wave of emotion through me as my knuckles tighten on the steering wheel.

I find Cade in my recent contacts and hit dial.

"Hey man!" he answers on the first ring.

"He's in the apartment!! He is attacking her!!"

I hear sirens turn on in the background and it sounds like he pushes the talk button on his radio. "Dispatch this is 459. I need all available units at 1059 Apartments. Home invasion, suspect is known to be violent. Female tenant is inside."

"Where are you!?" Cade asks coming back to the phone.

"I was on my way to my doctor's appointment. She was on her way to work. Lexi was picking her up and taking her. I am heading back now."

"Collin, don't get yourself killed trying to make it back."

"It's Alyssa, Cade! I have to get to her."

"We are right behind you man. Backup's coming." I hear dispatch in the background confirming units in route.

Hang on baby. Hang on.

My mind races with all the possible things he could do to her, and my fingers tighten their grip on the steering wheel.

I am ready to murder someone if that's the case.

Five minutes later, the wheels of Alyssa's car come to a halt at the front of her building. It doesn't seem like the cops have arrived yet.

Barreling out of the car, I run as fast as I can, not even caring about my leg, to the front door. Turning the handle and pushing it open, my eyes widen when I hear the sound of a gun firing, and I see Kyle falling to the floor.

Alyssa's eyes are hardened, and her body language rages with confidence. "Hey." I walk to her, calmly placing my hand over the pistol and lowering it down to her side. "Alyssa, look at me."

Her eyes finally move from his lifeless body to my eyes making her knees collapse as I catch her fall.

"He threatened our baby," she cries. "He threatened to undo it."

I hold her as the sound of sirens get closer; fear takes over me. I'm not sure how I am going to explain this, and hope Cade can help.

Cade's the first one inside and when he sees what is going on, he asks the other officers to stay out on the front lawns.

"Hey," he says calmly, walking up to Alyssa, smiling. "You, okay? Did he hurt you?"

His eyes roam over her body where some blood is oozing from scratches and a bruise forming on her head.

She shakes her head, "He was going to." Her eyes turn fearful, "Oh god, I killed him. Oh god, am I going to jail?"

My eyes find Cade's asking the same question without saying the words.

He takes a deep breath and lets it out slowly. "You may have to stand before a jury, but I think everything will work out. I will try my best to work the paperwork right."

A thought crosses my mind, making me grab my phone out of my pocket and pulling up the app. Sure enough, it worked.

I grin. "Cade, will this be enough to prove self-defense?" I hand him my phone with all the camera footage from the incident.

Last week, I put in new cameras on the outside of the apartment, but I also put some on the inside. Alyssa was not aware of the inside ones, and I wanted to keep it that way. I knew there would come a time I would have to leave her, and she would be on her own; in case that happened, I wanted to have a way to see the inside of the apartment.

Alyssa looks at me shockingly. "Collin. You thought of everything."

I kiss her forehead. "I wanted a Plan B, just in case."

Cade stands, "This will be enough to completely close the case. You will be just fine," he assures us before walking outside and handing me my phone back.

Hitting play, I watch the event unfold. The son of a bitch was sitting in the parking lot before I left and waited until I had been gone a little while before entering. Once inside, he went straight to the bathroom to make his presence known.

My hand makes a fist as I watch him attack my girl.

"Collin, don't do this to yourself. It's over." Alyssa's hands go to my chest.

But I need to see it. I need to watch until the end.

'Didn't you get my flowers of congratulations? It's okay. I'll forgive you once I get rid of it.'

Our baby.

"Collin, I had no choice." Alyssa looks at me teary eyed. "He wouldn't have stopped."

"Shhh." I grab her close to me as officers and other people start coming in to get Kyle's dead body. "You did what you had to do. It was self-defense. None of this is your fault."

"Can we check you out?" a man in a medic uniform comes up and kneels by Alyssa's feet. "I can put some medicine on those scratches and see about getting a CT for that bruise."

"She is pregnant," I tell him, and his eyes widen. "Yes, please come with me. We need to have you checked out at the hospital. Are you her husband?" he looks at me.

Alyssa smiles. "He will be." He is the father of my baby.

***

We left Cade and his coworkers to clean up the mess while the ambulance took Alyssa to the hospital. I followed along behind them in her car so when she gets discharged, we will be able to come home.

"Collin!" Lexie yells from the parking lot when I pull in, running toward me. "Is she okay? Oh my god, I was running late because my stupid gas tank was on empty."

"She is shaken up but okay. We are just having her and the baby checked out," I assure her as we both walk to the ER entrance.

"Collin Mapleson." A familiar voice makes me smile when Becky comes into sight. "She is this way, follow me."

Becky has been a good friend of the family's for years and knowing she here makes a few bricks weighing on my chest ease off.

"I remember when you were just a baby and now here you are, having your own." She grins at me. "She is in room 102." She gestures to the door and walks back to the nurse's station.

Swinging the door open, I walk over to the hospital bed, grabbing my girl's hand and holding it tight. "You feeling okay?"

She smiles. "Yes." Her eyes fall behind me to Lexie, who now has tears flooding her face.

"I am so sorry. I was running late," She walks to the other side of the hospital bed and grabs Alyssa's other hand.

"I am glad you weren't there," Alyssa tells her. "He would have hurt you too."

"But you have a little one to worry about. He could have hurt me if it meant you and the little bean were okay."

Alyssa tears up. "I am forever thankful for your friendship. I love you, Lex."

"I love you." Lexie's tears continue to fall.

"Knock Knock." The door opens, an older middle-aged man walks in wearing a lab coat and smiles. "You are extremely lucky," he tells Alyssa. "And by the way, your baby is perfectly fine."

Alyssa's head falls back on the pillow and tears of relief leak out. My eyes blurred some too.

Looking up to the ceiling I mouth, "Thank you." I am sure my parents, grandparents, and uncle had a helping hand in today.

"What about your leg?" Alyssa asks randomly.

I chuckle. "I have cleared myself. I ran from the parking lot to the apartment. No pain and no discomfort." I dance around in a circle making Alyssa smile.

Chapter Thirty-Two
Alyssa

It's later afternoon before they release me from the ER. The bump on my head meant they wanted to keep me for observation a few hours in case of a concussion and to run some fluids in me.

Lexie left not long after she and Collin arrived—if I am being honest, Collin had to pry her off me and make her leave. She feels guilty for not being here with me.

Collin pulls us out onto the main road, grabbing my hand and placing it in his lap, but releases it shortly when his phone starts to ring.

"Hey man, everything good? We are heading back now."

"What?" he yells and whips the car in the direction of Maple.

"Magnolia Farm is on fire," he says worriedly. "From what Cade could hear on the scanner, a firefighter has run inside because someone was inside the house, and it is fully engulfed."

"Oh my god, Collin," I gasp. "Put your flashers on and drive faster!"

He hits the flasher button and stomps the gas, throwing me back in my seat and zooming in and out of traffic.

"I need this fucking day to be over," he huffs out.

I close my eyes, praying that Cade misunderstood and no one is inside.

Usually, Maple is a fifteen-minute drive from Cedartown, but we made it in ten. Pulling on the Magnolia Farm driveway, we could already see the black smoke and the lights of first responder vehicles at the end of the road.

"Collin." My heart sinks.

"Don't let it be them. Don't let it be them." He rocks in his seat.

As we end the straight driveway and come closer to the house, Maggie and Logan are the first two we notice.

Collin puts the car in park behind one of the fire trucks and we both jump out running to the house. "Maggie!" Collin says, getting her attention and she runs up to us, wiping tears and throws her arms around Collin. "Megan was inside. She is okay. Derek got her out."

Collin tries to balance himself before his legs give out and I place my hand on his back. "Maggie said she is okay Collin."

Maggie walks off toward the ambulance and Logan pulls Collin into a hug. "You look like shit," he jokes and Collin grins. "So do you."

Where am I going to live now? Megan's voice is heard coming from the back of the ambulance and we walk around to the opening in the back.

"She acts like she doesn't own all this land." Collin smiles up at his sister who looks happy and relieved to see him—and us.

He jumps up in the back with her and hugs her tight. Walking out of the back and back beside me, Maggie hugs him again too.

Megan reaches out her hand again and Collin squeezes it. "I am glad you are okay."

"Me too." She grins at both of us.

Derek walks up beside us and Collin puts his hand on his back, getting his attention before mouthing, "Thank you."

"Anyone riding with us?" the medic asks, and Derek jumps in the back.

"Am I missing something?" Collin asks when the medic closes the door and drives off.

I lean into him. "They are doing doggy style."

I think he might puke for a minute before he shrugs. "If that's what makes her less moody, I will happily encourage all the doggy style in the world."

I roll my eyes. "Nothing fazes you, does it?"

Logan and Maggie start hoarse laughing.

"You got a lot to learn about him if you don't already know that." Maggie giggles.

***

It's been a few days since the home invasion from Kyle and the fire at Magnolia Farms. We haven't told anyone about the Kyle thing right now and Cade promised he try his best to keep it under wraps.

Eventually, we will tell everyone, but right now I think we just want to take the time to understand everything that has happened this week and regulate our emotions.

Megan is still in the hospital, so Collin and I decided today we would go visit her and Derek.

"You want to tell them about the baby?" Collin asks on our way there.

We haven't told them about the pregnancy either. It is not that we didn't want to, it was just all bad timing. When we first found out, I wanted to make sure everything was okay with it, and we weren't going to lose it.

Then when the fire happened—the timing was just bad.

As much as I want this little one known about, I am terrified of what people may think too.

Collin and I have not been together that long, and this was a sudden surprise.

"Nah." I smile. "Let Megan get home first and then we can."

He nods with a grin. "I will support that."

Entering the hospital, I notice something immediately; my anxiety is gone.

A place that used to hold such nightmares for me has turned into a place of second chances.

Yes, this is where I got the final news about my sister, but it's also the place that saved Collin's life and the place that told me our baby was still thriving.

How could I not be grateful for such success? We all have bad things happening in our life. But we also have choices; to let it consume us and keep us from truly living or push forward and continue living despite all the bad.

The elevator ascends to the third floor, and we step off, turning left down a hallway to room number 304—at least that's where Derek texted Collin to go.

"Knock Knock," I say, opening the door to the room and hear someone say, "Collin, she has a surprise for—" but Megan puts her hands up and slams her phone on the table beside her hospital bed.

Derek's laugh breaks out across the room making Collin and I both raise an eyebrow in question.

"What was that?" Collin asks.

"Everything okay?" I question behind him.

She and Derek both grin at one another and look back at us. Megan speaks, "How do you guys feel about being an aunt and uncle?" She twirls the bottom of her hair while Collin and I look at each other in shock.

Collin nods at me and I smile back. "Depends. How do you guys feel about being an aunt and uncle too? That is, if you are together again or not." I laugh but Megan rolls her eyes.

"W-wait." Megan sits up in her bed, her eyes finding Derek's. He is just as curious as she is. "You're not pregnant, are you?"

All I can do is nod with tears in my eyes.

So much for waiting to tell everyone, I laugh to myself.

"Are you?" I finally ask her.

All Megan can do is nod with tears too.

"How far along are you?" she asks me but Collin answers, "Doctor says about seven weeks."

"We are five." Derek says excitedly. Collin and he both embrace in a giant man hug.

I run over to Megan's hospital bed and bear hug her too.

"Some groveling he did," I smirk at her.

When I stand up, wiping tears, Derek engulfs me in a bear hug too, making me cry even more. This is a hug I have needed for a year now. I have missed him being in my life. And my sister would love Megan.

"She's good for you," I whisper to him. "Haley would be happy knowing you have Megan."

"Thanks Alyssa," he says through his tears, his voice hoarse. "Kind of crazy we could be in-laws again someday."

Megan exclaims, "We have to facetime Maggie, or she will kill us keeping all of this from her."

I look at Collin and nod silently, telling him we need to go tell them on our own. "We are going when we leave here." He smiles at me.

For the first time since I have met her, this feels like the perfect beginning of a beautiful friendship between Megan and me.

Chapter Thirty-Three
Collin

"I cannot wait to see little Rhett again." Alyssa beams beside me in the passenger seat.

The farmhouse—well, what used to be a farmhouse—comes into view as we ride down the long driveway toward Logan and Maggie's house.

A pain hits my chest seeing the rubble all over the ground. The remainder of the house is smoldering on the ground with smoke billowing from the center.

Memories of my childhood flash rapidly through my mind, making my vison blur through tears.

"Hey." Alyssa's arm goes to my shoulder. "You want to stop?"

I nod and pull up to where the front porch used to be. The dogs run up to us and I can tell they are confused. The porch they used to sleep on is now gone.

"Hey guys," I say, bending down and patting all their heads. "It's okay. It'll all be okay."

Standing back up, Alyssa's arm wraps around my side, pulling herself closer into me. My arm drapes around her back and I laugh to keep the tears from flowing. "Used to think I would live here forever. In the same room, eat out of the same kitchen, and walk those same stairs every day." I point to the stairs that now lay flat on the ground—well, parts of them.

"I remember one time grandma caught me riding down those stairs on my bicycle. She had been gone to the market and grandfather was out checking fences with Megan. I thought I was grown, though I was only probably ten at the time. Grandma walked in about the time I was coming down the stairs and she moved just in time for me to head out the door onto the front porch and down the porch steps," I chuckle. "Scared the shit out of me and her."

Alyssa giggles beside me. "Sounds like you had a wonderful childhood."

"I want our child to experience the same." I lean down and kiss her softly. "Come on, let's go see Maggie and Logan."

I always loved where Maggie and Logan built their home. A beautiful white farmhouse with a wonderful view of the sunset. Logan stands on the front porch when we pull up, drinking a glass of tea.

"Well, well, well," he smirks. "Look who is walking without crutches."

I grin, walking up on the porch and throw my arms around him. "Look who is getting grey hair," I joke.

He huffs. "Just wait until you have a little one. The stress is unreal."

He turns to Alyssa and smiles. "I still don't know how you put up with him."

She smiles, hugging him. "I got him trained well."

"Ha!" Maggie steps out on the porch, holding Rhett. "Please tell me you used a shock collar."

"Hey!" I run up and hug my cousin and smile at Rhett.

Pulling out of our hug, Maggie's teary eyes hold mine. "Nothing was salvageable. We tried this morning. Everything is gone." She holds Rhett out for Logan to hold and walks back into the house, returning with a paper and chains wrapped around her hand. "Sit." She gestures to the swing. She, Alyssa, and I all take a seat.

"I did find this. It knocked the breath out of my lungs when I found it. It was under some rubble and lying beside it was grandfather's dog tags from the war." She opens her hands and hands me the dog tags. "He would want you to have them. Pass them down to your child someday."

Alyssa's hand goes to my knee, and it takes everything inside me to fight back the tears forming. "And this." Maggie unfolds the paper. "It was in perfect condition, like it had never been in the fire to begin with."

She hands it to me wiping a tear.

Keep dodging those curveballs.

I lose the strength to keep it together. The past few days have been emotional and seeing my grandmother's famous words breaks the floodgates.

Maggie leans her head over on me and we cry together; even Logan is wiping tears.

Once the tears subside, I grab Alyssa's hand. "I guess our little one is getting dog tags."

Logan's eyes widen and Maggie jumps out of the swing. "Are you?" she points to Alyssa.

Alyssa nods with a soft smile.

"Oh my god!!!" she squeals. "You and Megan?" She covers her mouth. "Oh shit."

I laugh. "We know. They told us before we came here."

She lets out a breath. "Whew. Good."

"That means we get to try for a second." Logan winks at Maggie making us giggle and Maggie's cheeks turn red.

***

Logan, Maggie, Rhett, Alyssa, and I stand where the front porch used to be, waiting on Derek and Megan to arrive. She has been discharged from the hospital and Derek texted Logan not too long ago, alerting us that they were on their way.

Alyssa grabs my hand, pulling me close to her. "Let's say we get out of that small apartment and start our forever home."

"Are you sure you are ready for that?" I ask.

"Collin, I want our baby to grow up with his or her cousins. I want our baby to have the same memories and childhood you had. I want them to feel the love living here will bring them."

My lips meet hers gently. "Ready when you are."

The sound of tires on gravel gets all of our attention as dust flies behind Derek's truck. "Our girl's home." Maggie squeezes my shoulder making me grin.

Once the truck stops outside the house, Logan and I walk around to help Megan out.

"Feeling okay?" Logan asks, taking her hand.

"I cannot believe my stupid self lit that candle." Her voice breaks. Maggie walks over and puts her arm around Megan. "What matters is that you and sweet little peanut are okay."

Maggie and Megan walk slowly to where the front of the house used to be. I slowly make my way up behind them, my arm going around their shoulders.

The three of us look at what used to be and all the memories we have made. Rhett cries, getting our attention. "Hand him to me." Maggie says to Logan.

I reach my hand out to Alyssa, pulling her into the other side of me.

Protecting what's Mine

Our past might only be memories now, but it's the future I look the most forward to. Raising the next generation of Mapleson kiddos is going to be the best years of our lives.

Epilogue
Alyssa

A year has passed since the fire at Magnolia Farm and my home invasion with Kyle.

To say I am okay now is the understatement of the century, but moving out to the farm was the best thing we ever did.

A few weeks before we moved, I would have nightmares. The doctor said pregnancy tends to increase vivid and out of the ordinary dreams, and since I had endured a trauma too, my mind was trying to process it all. He even encouraged the move saying, 'getting out of the environment that caused the trauma would be good.'

Collin took him so seriously that when we came home that day, he loaded all my shit in the back of his truck, making multiple trips and moved us. That night, we were sleeping in Logan's old apartment above the barn.

Megan and Derek moved into Maggie and Logan's house for about a week until Derek showed up with an RV for them, saying he needed time alone with his girl.

I quit my job at the diner—which made Lexie sad, but we still see her and Cade often.

They like to visit us from time to time at the farm, especially since Cash has been born.

Jeffrey Cash Mapleson has been the missing piece of the puzzle in my life, and I almost missed out on him.

I think back often to the day I decided I was going to end it all; the grief and trauma was just too much to hold onto and it makes me feel guilty that I almost took away the chance for my life to change—for the better.

I would have never met Collin, his family, Magnolia Farm, or my precious baby boy.

I would have never fallen in love all over again watching my cowboy become a daddy.

Walking out onto our front porch, our chocolate lab, Hero, runs out past me into the yard making his way into the pasture to play with the other dogs.

Collin swings in the bed swing on the right, Cash in his arms as the evening sun sets around the mountains.

"Hey Daddy," I smile, walking over to them, handing Collin a bottle and settling in beside my two greatest joys in life.

"Hey Mama." Collin grins, grabbing the bottle from me and feeding Cash.

"How was your nap?" he asks me.

I smile. Collin has gone above and beyond since Cash's delivery, allowing me to rest and take naps when I feel overwhelmed. He helps with late night feedings and is the most present dad.

"It was fantastic. Thank you for taking all the weight of the world off my shoulders." I lean my head over on him.

"If more men would understand nothing is more important than home and family, there would be fewer broken homes," he says honestly.

"I don't know what I ever did to deserve you, Mr. Mapleson but I sure am thankful."

He turns, his body facing me and says, 'Which reminds me. Cash has a question for you."

I raise an eyebrow, "Collin, he cannot talk yet."

He chuckles. "His shirt."

I look down and it takes a moment for my brain to catch up with the words I am reading.

Hey mommy. Will you marry my daddy?

My eyes dart to Collin and he uses his free hand to bring something out from behind his back. It's a black jewelry box. "You will have to open it since my other hand is tied up."

I laugh, grabbing it from him and opening the box to find a beautiful square-cut diamond ring inside.

Tears flood my cheeks and drip off my chin. "Yes," I whisper. "Yes, I will marry your daddy," I coo at Cash.

"You hear that buddy? She said yes! I told you there was nothing to be nervous about," Collin says to Cash, making me giggle. He uses his free hand to take the ring out of the box and place it on my wedding ring finger.

"I am sure Cash was anxious about it." I wink.

"He almost threw up," Collin assures me with wide eyes.

"Is that so?" I tease.

"Which reminds me," he starts. "When can I tell him about doggy style?"

I huff. "Collin Mapleson, I swear to god!"

"I think you actually did that when Cash was conceived too," he mocks me.

My hand slaps his shoulder, and he says, "Hey. No violence when I have the baby."

Out of the corner of my eye, something red gets my attention.

Five cardinals sit on the dogwood tree branch right out from the porch. I am not sure how long they have been there, but they all watch us; one of them lets out a chirp.

"Well, I'll be," Collin starts. "I always heard cardinals are passed loved ones visiting you from heaven."

My eyes water again with tears. If that's so then Haley, Collin's grandparents, and his parents were all here and present for our engagement. I have seen them a lot lately.

"You believe in that stuff?" I ask him.

He nods. "You got to believe in something or else you'll fall for anything."

Epilogue Two
Collin
Sixteen years later

The sound of a truck cranking wakes me from a deep sleep. I nudge Alyssa in the side, "Hey pretty girl. Wake up."

"What?" she grumbles.

"I think Cash has snuck out again."

"Ugh." She throws the covers over her head as I do the same. "This kid is going to be the death of me."

I chuckle. "Tell me about it."

Alyssa jumps when her phone starts to ring. "Hello?" she answers. "Yes, we just heard the truck leave." Her eyes find mine and I know that look all too well.

The other cousins have snuck out too.

She puts her phone on speaker and throws it to the bed while she changes out of her nightclothes.

"Kimber has left the gate open that leads to the barn." Megan's voice doesn't sound happy at all. "Derek is on the phone with Logan now. Sounds like Rhett is gone too."

"Can they at least stay home and not drive off when they get a wild hair?" I speak out loud. "I know we did stupid shit Meg, but at least we stayed on the farm."

"I told you I hoped my child didn't act like you. She is the ringleader of the three of them," she chuckles.

"Horseback or trucks?" Alyssa asks, wanting to know how we are going to look for them.

We hear Derek in the background. "Horseback and four-wheeler. I have a hunch where they are."

"And how do you know?" Megan asks while still on the phone.

"Because I overheard Kimber earlier taking about the back forty."

"Meg, we can cover more ground with the horses. Alyssa, ride with Derek on the Ranger and we will meet at the back creek."

"Okay." They say in unison.

Maggie and Logan meet us at the barn too. Saddling up our horses, we cousins mount our horses while our spouses slide into the Ranger and follow back behind us.

"While I want to express how they need to stop doing this and be safe, I also am thankful these three have one another," Maggie smiles. "If I had been around for my childhood, I am sure we would have done the same thing.

Megan smiles, "We would have given Collin hell."

I roll my eyes, "Like you don't now."

Crossing the creek, we see a flashlight off in the distance making us kick the horses into a gallop toward it.

That's when my heart does a summersault in my chest. Our kids have crossed the main creek, to the back side of the pasture. Where Logan killed the coyote the first time Maggie came to the farm.

"What are they doing?" Maggie's voice worried. "They crossed the creek. They know better than that!"

That's one of the few rules we have given them over the years—the creek is off limits.

The kids spot us and start screaming. All it takes is to hear the words, "HELP!" before adrenaline rushes through me, making me cross the creek to get to our kids. Megan and Maggie are right behind me.

Once on the other side, we kick the horses again into a gallop and reach the pasture line.

"I left my phone at home. We couldn't leave them alone." Kimber's voice is hoarse.

She holds a newborn calf in her arms. Mama cow is lying dead beside her.

"We tried to save mama, but the baby was breeched." Cash says. I now notice blood covers him from his shoulders to his hands.

"We tried so damn hard," Rhett's voice is barely above a whisper, his voice trembling.

The kids have worked many similar scenarios on the farm with us, but never alone. They have always had one of us with them. The fact that they stayed calm and worked as hard as they could to have the best possible outcome makes pride swell in my chest.

"The baby needs colostrum or it's going to die." Kimber's big heart is so much like her mother's. The love she has for these animals is astonishing.

The Ranger pulls up behind us and our spouses get out, rushing over, and taking in the scene.

"Here," Derek says, leaning down and grabbing the calf from Kimber.

"No daddy. I'm not leaving her."

"Okay. Then how about you ride back with Uncle Logan and Aunt Alyssa? I will ride your horse back. You can sit in the middle with the calf and hold her until we can get her inside the house and warmed up."

She nods and lets him help her stand.

Placing my hand on Cash's and Rhett's shoulder I pull them into me, "Fine job boys. Fine job. I am so proud of you." I look back at Kimber, "All of you."

The truth is, I now know what my grandfather meant by the beauty of this land and the things these animals could teach you. I know why his greatest desire was for it to be ours one day—he wanted that next generation to take it on and let it teach them.

Now I am certain the generation after us will continue the legacy we have continued ourselves.

Protecting what's Mine

Acknowledgments

To my husband, thank you for being a Collin in my life of dealing with a Kyle. You saw me in some of my darkness days and brought a flashlight to lead me to the light again. Collin's comedy is from you. Thank you for always making me laugh the way Collin makes Alyssa laugh. I love you.

To my ARC readers, THANK YOU for taking a chance on a baby Author. Your support in me is what kept me going in a time of imposter syndrome and doubt.

To my PA, Paige, I wish I could pay you a thousand times what I do. I am so thankful our paths crossed.

To all my Readers, THANK YOU from the bottom of my heart. For every review, pages read, books bought, messages, social media post, and more. I have been overwhelmed at the support you all have given me. One day I hope to hug your necks.

Protecting what's Mine

Follow Jessica's socials

Instagram: @jessicawhaleybooks
Tiktok: @jessicawhaleybooks
Website: authorjdwhaley.com